Lion's Gra
and Other Stories

Nunatak Fiction

Nunatak is an Inuktitut word meaning "lonely peak"; a rock or mountain rising above ice. During Quaternary glaciation in North America these peaks stood above the ice sheet and so became refuges for plant and animal life. Magnificent nunataks, their bases scoured by glaciers, can be seen along the Highwood Pass in the Alberta Rocky Mountains and on Ellesmere Island.

Nunataks are especially selected works of outstanding fiction by new western writers. The editors of Nunataks for NeWest Press are Aritha van Herk and Rudy Wiebe.

Lion's Granddaughter and Other Stories

Yasmin Ladha

NeWest Press, Edmonton

First Edition

Canadian Cataloguing in Publication Data

Ladha, Yasmin.
Lion's granddaughter and other stories

(Nunatak fiction)
ISBN 0-920897-25-8

I. Title. II. Series.
PS8573.A2798L5 1992 C813'.54 C92-091456-X
PR9199.3.L32L5 1992

CREDITS:
Cover Design: Diane Jensen
Cover Photo: Robin Silver Jensen
Interior Design: John Luckhurst/Graphic Design Limited
Editor for the Press: Aritha van Herk
Financial Assistance: NeWest Press gratefully acknowledges the financial assistance of Alberta Culture and Multiculturalism, The Alberta Foundation for the Arts, The Canada Council, and The NeWest Institute for Western Canadian Studies.

Printed and bound in Canada by Best Gagné Book Manufacturers

NeWest Publishers Limited
Suite 310, 10359 - 82 Avenue
Edmonton, Alberta
T6E 1Z9

This is a book of fiction and all characters are fictional.

For Fabai

I would like to express my gratitude to my teachers Fred Wah, Chris Wiseman, and Aritha van Herk, in whose workshops I really began to write; the Faculty of Environmental Design for allowing me the use of its facilities and where many of these pieces began; funding from the Alberta Foundation for the Literary Arts and the ATJ Cairns Scholarship in the completion of this project; Sharon La Frenz for her copious help; Syed Shah for all the help in India; and Fatma Ladha for waiting up for me.

Contents

My teacher's ashram
has no thatched roof, turquoise peacock or banyan tree
her office
6th floor of Craigie Hall
where two Mars bars, side by side: lunch
my teacher of green eyes, coyote shape
(I swear this is not a cliche)
half her pupil
turns murky brown in her mantra:
pupa, pupil, push.

Beena

Readerji, you have never wanted me forever
But this time
Won't you come a little farther?

I shan't call you reader. One who reads, hah! That's so undeclared. Blank as a daft blue form: "Resident of?" "In the Dominion of?" "Port of Embarkation/Disembarkation?" "Destitute-Festitute?" Blue muscle of power. Generic.

Between you and me, there is no glint of a badge. Badges are razor sharp. Between you and me, the ink quivers. Beena exists declared (fetch the trumpet, fetch the *dholak: dha dhin dhinaka*) because of you and me.

"*A* reader," you say? You correcting me? My Allah! You have joined the critic's English! May he forever be buried in the Sahara. *Readerji*, I command you, banish the critic from your eye, this instant, *fatafat!* Look at his beauty nose, wide as a camel's nostrils!

My *yaar-Readerji*, sometimes with my own, I forget this definite and not so definite article stuff. Allah! You are turning gray because I call you my own! *Readerji*, by bending, yes-Masta, yes-Masta, you follow the colonizer-critic to his bed!

You and me: Our relationship is declared and you are off to the Camel-*wallah's* bed. *La!* I am breaking my bangles, because of you, *you Readerji*. You have made me a widow. Wait, I will even wipe off my red-*bindi*, this moon-dot between my eyebrows, my *shakti*-power. And the vermilion from my hair parting. *Readerji*, you are turning a nastier gray. You frighten me. Oh, I frighten you? No need to be so vehement with your nod. This *maha* critic's sun never sets, not even a wheezy sound of setting. You, breaker of my bangles, salaaming with yes-Masta, yes-Masta deference. *Readerji*, I ask you, will the critic's privilege, his Brahmin privilege, will it never cease? You are content to drink the incantations from his *soma* drink? He works on formulas while I, my precious reader, create. Without you *Readerji*, my *shakti*-power is swollen but my text is a widow, *gum-sum*/quiet-quiet/sawdust. So. So. So. Fill my arms with green, green bangles, *Readerji*. From you, my hefty fertility. And the critic/Brahmin/camel/colonizer is out, out of text! *Readerji*, Beena *soma*-wine, yours-mine, *salut!* That needly bone in my kabab is the critic. So I have the camel-nostril-*wallah* mincemeated in a yellow plastic bowl. Do you know *Readerji*, I make lovely kababs, full of garlic and wet coriander? You would lick your fingers dry. Now this is religion. Only the critic's nostrils put me off.

Come *Readerji*, sit on my bed where I write. Make cool circles on the sheet with the heel of your foot. I dream of a study with pipe smoke and wooden floor (so briskly polished you want to wear your hair up). No colonizing table with loopy gold handles and filched Koh-i-Noors. Just rosewood mailboxes one finds in old fashioned hotels. But *Readerji*, dreams aside, I write here, on this bed. Have some carrot *achar* on *chapatti*. No my precious Reader, these are not green chilies, just peppers. Beena loves carrot *achar*. Your eyes have grown large. Why can't you accept you are declared in Beena? Don't smell my ink in the critic's nostril. I have a heart beat too.

Such a hoard of treasure I lay before you, yet you read like a *fakir*. A critic's *fakir*. Living off his scraps. Hey, don't leave me to my new-found independence! What do you mean I am scaring the shit out of you? Even I am unaccustomed to popping in and out of pages with *achar* and *chai*.

Careful, the *chai* is hot. Sugar? Only half a teaspoon? No wonder you are so disciplined. I take one, two, and finally three teaspoons of sugar. I like syrup in my throat. *Readerji*, trust me. No, I should not say this. At least, not when I am with Satya.

How do you know that *satya* means truth? Oh, the Gandhi film. Well, my dear friend's lies would send firecrackers up Gandhiji's ass, may his soul rest in peace.

One day on the C-Train, this friendly man comes up to us, Satya and me. Asks if we are sisters? Satya tells him, "We have the same mother but different fathers." And when the friendly man, now red, turns to me, Satya adds, "Oh, she's the bastard."

Readerji, this frown of yours is breaking Satya's magic. Her tongue is lightning. Satya in Beena's story? Faintly, I guess. *Readerji*, hood your glaring eye. There is never only *a* story. That's why a story's collar bones are chubby (always) because she carries layers and layers of stories.

Satya is my *sakhi*, my dearest friend. We hang rainbow saris on rooftops and fetch water from the well. *Ooi Readerji*, will you now forget the C-Train? Stand clear of the doors. And imagine a century where women wear pleated *lenga* skirts with tiny *bindi*-shaped mirrors around the hem. The skirts blast with colour, violent pink on orange, and green on pollen yellow. Each doorway arch painted with tendril leaves and parrots and water pitchers. The outside walls stamped with the orange benevolent elephant God. At doorsteps, coloured rice powder in sprawling circular patterns.

From the discreet *jharoka*, two *sakhis* stare out into the town square. One is a writer, the *Pen-walli*. The other is Satya, the *zenana* law-breaker.

"In this slumbering afternoon, not even a crow in sight," says *Pen-walli*.

"I want *paan*."

"Satya, *Amma* will eat us raw."

"Only if she finds out. Don't know how a timid rabbit like you is a writer. Ring for *Maharaj* of the Kitchen."

"The *Maharaj*, here! In the *zenana!* But all the women are sleeping and he will look in on each one of them!"

"That's why *pronto, fatafat*, he will rush to the female quarters. *Maha* opportunity for *Maharaj* to let his eyes slip on slumbering beauties."

Knock. Knock.

"*Bibijis*, you remembered me."

"*Nahi Maharaj*, it is we who remembered you."

"*Salaam*, Satyaji, friend of our *Pen-bibiji*."

"*Maharaj*, there is not a just word for this afternoon's yogurt lamb sauce and your *halva* full of blanched almonds, *hai* Allah, all my words have lost elasticity."

"Lady Satyaji, and my bow grows insufficient in light of such praise. Bestow a command, my way."

"But I have not finished, *Maharaj*. I swear in the presence of my writer *sakhi*, if you are lifted one fine day and find your auspicious self in the humble kitchen of our *haveli*, you must relieve me of any blame. You are a Koh-i-Noor meant to be stolen."

"Satyaji, your *haveli* is the Grand Palace of our city."

"Then, dear *Maharaj*, I hope you will not refuse the request of the dweller of the Grand Palace."

"Your wish is my command, daughter of the Grand Palace."

"*Maharaj*, you are forwarding us your precious tongue."

"Indeed, my treasured organ on which spices punch and dance."

"Then *Maharaj*, the secret mariner of sauces, maintainer of heirloom secrets, I bid you to fetch us *paan*, and an attached favour, spittoons from the male quarters."

Readerji, now our *Maharaj* is Shinto calm. Not a crack in his eye. He has given his word. But he is a professional tongue shaker in more than just the Bengali fish *pilaff* way:

"Hot or sweet, O *cleverest* daughter of the Grand Palace?"

"*Maharaj* of the Kitchen, if I were a lamb, my throat would be at your disposal — awaiting on your stone slab. But today, the *zenana* rules, made possible of course, by your lavish promise. *Sweet-ta paan* with fragrant red paste for my writer *sakhi*. In mine, a hefty pinch of tobacco. And I must reiterate I have the honour of your tongue."

"O Grand Palace one, I have been groomed by *haveli* nobility. To consume an ocean of secrets without a burp is my *dharma*."

"*Cookji*, and if you would indulge us further — a small *taklif*-imposition on our behalf. . . ."

"Clever one, my pound of flesh at your service."

"Dear *Cookji*, then if you would *purdah* your eyes on your way out, how can I say? As an extension of your *dharma*-duty, if you please."

Satya and *Pen-walli* sit on the balcony on this slumbering afternoon. They rest their henna-painted feet on ice-wrapped cushions, their spittoons close by. Actually, of the two, the writer is the smart spitter. From her lightly bulged cheeks, the betel juice forms a red-rusty arc and lands unspilt in the silver receiver engraved with a cheetah chasing a deer. (*Readerji*, engraved on a courtesan's spittoon is an arched woman holding a mirror.)

Readerji, now what's the matter? Even you should know that courtesans never do things plainly. Anyway, the most important event in the history of story-telling is about to occur. Out with the *dholak: dhum dhum dhaa aha, dhum dhum dhaa.* (Forget the dictionary tom-tom — drums of India and West Indies, hah! Then I can only think of Tom of peep holes who peep-peeping so fast becomes Tom-Tom.) Twirling fingers swift on the drum, and the palm-beat, *dhumaka dhumaka dhaa.* LISTEN ONE AND ALL: *Readerji* IS ABOUT TO ENTER THE STORY.

Ooi Readerji, where are you off to? If you run away, how will I continue with the story? You will come to no harm, I swear on the story. You don't trust the story. How can I coax you to step in? You want no knotted embrace with the courtesan? Agreed. *Readerji*, tell me, what if I plan her *haveli* by a lake? Not possible, you say? You figure that her brothel is most likely behind the *paan-wallah's* shop. Of course, *Readerji!* One lucrative trade massages another. You co-create very logically, *Readerji*, but this is no city planning course. I like the idea of a languorous boat ride. Okay, okay, I won't put you on a boat ride with her. Why do you get so worked up? But *ooi* my friend, in the story, you have such style.

Satya sees you first.

"What a walk! Allah, thank you for releasing him, our way!"

The *Pen-walli* is content spittoon spitting. Now she ogles at you. *Readerji*, this time, she forgets to let out the proper cheek pressure and the juice lands on her bodice.

As you are about to pass under their balcony, Satya and *Pen-walli* bend over.

Only Satya clutches her heart. "*Hai hai*, what a city walk! What a cut in this lurch of a walk!"

My proper *Readerji*, rub away that hairpin frown of yours, for you *would* look up, I swear. Because Satya has ropy power. It pulls you. Look up, look back, heck, look anywhere you please. In this story, you won't turn to stone. Ah! You too are drawn to her voice. I know, I know, there lies a pressed thickness in it. Ah yes, you do look up, definitely.

(*Readerji*, shshsh! Just between you and me, you have that

certain walk. It is a walk that finishes one like Emma Bovary's eyes.)

Readerji, do you want to see your picture in words? Sleek silk pantaloons. Not those billowy village pyjamas. Pantaloons and the embroidered belt, just above the hips, have a language of their own. They slice forward with a hint of a buck, while your hair jolts back, like wings at a terrific speed.

Ooi, now I see that I have lost my reputation with you. *Nahi Readerji*, I have never observed your walk this minutely. Don't pull your collar any higher, for I am not a courtesan. My microscopic eye is words.

Readerji, for a change, let me ask you a question? Why *Beena* from all the other books choked with dust (but oh so patient) on the tenth floor of the Library Tower?

The name pulled you. I told you, I create magic, my precious. Certainly, Beena is not of the common Safeway variety. Do you know there was once a filmstar in the fifties and her name was Beena? No, no, our Beena doesn't become an actress. But you asked! I have not given away anything! Then what is a Safeway and a filmstar doing in an Indian village where women wash their clothes by the river? Hey *Readerji*, where did you get these details? Imagination! Good for you. (May the critic forever remain in a yellow plastic bowl.) But did I mention a river? Yes, I know I mention a boat which you don't want to share with a courtesan. Ah! this reminds you of *Kama Sutra*. Oh no, don't turn shy *Readerji*, please go on. You say that *Kama Sutra* brings forth positions which you allow yourself to conjure only with the condition that a chiropractor's office is in visible proximity. And figs and a river, of course. *Readerji*, co-create Beena with me but don't be disappointed. You see, there is no *Kama Sutran* gymnast in this story. No, no, I am not patronizing you. I want to set the story straight, on my part at least. Oh this mad hairpin frown of yours. I know what it means. Don't bang the book shut, you will chop off my nose, I swear.

Readerji, may I speak the truth? *Nahi* what I told you before is also the truth, but now truth at the balcony level. What nonsense! What do you mean I am doing transcendental hocus pocus on you? No, I am not transmitting you to the Himalayas. Of course, I know you are not a California reader. Reader, my Reader, slow-slow. Tell me, what does an image of a balcony convey to you?

Ooi Readerji, how could you? I see Him, The Only Mr. Pen, Mr. *Vilayat* — Great UK, Mr. #1 name in the Canon, top-top English, zoomed on your forehead. He is in his famous tutu pantaloons laden with oval-nosed conceit. This famous Mr. *Pen-wallah's* balcony hogs other balconies in literature. Rub Him off! *Pronto! Fatafat!* Away with the Romeo and Juliet blinkers. Give this lovers' balcony a deserved break, au revoir, heart-bye, foot-bye, bye-bye, for ever! *Yaar*, there are other balconies too and other love stories, like Heer and Ranjha. In the desert, Heer shrieked for her lost Ranjha. There are some shrieks which can't be described. Heer's was such a shriek that God in heaven shook and descended instead. And Heer said to the Almighty Bufferer, "But you are not my Ranjha!"

Yaar-Reader, balconies remind me of the *balcony level truth*. It is difficult to explain. When it happens, you don't know if it happened or not because it is a scratch, an instant recognition, clutching, and then a black out. Finished. Balcony level truth "pings." It hits you privately, in the eye or stomach. (Yes, yes I acknowledge you are not a California reader.) Okay *Readerji*, let me explain. On television, I see a veiled woman hurrying down the street. For the first time, she is voting for a woman leader. At the ballot box, the woman extends her wrist, uncovering rose bangles. The "ping" for me isn't her vote for Benezir Bhutto as much as her rose bangles excited, out of black *purdah* shroud, out of prison. This "ping" and I write "Muslim Woman Pictures."

My friend paints women
rib-eyed
excavation stiff.
She strokes them patiently
hardening black paint
head to heel.
Nostrils flicked shut.
On top of their hood skulls
she fastens
wingy birds.

Readerji, you and me on the balcony. Eye-lash, heart-beat, itch-scratch, Be-eena. I am because you are. No, *Readerji*, no need to giddy up to the parasitic critic. There is no hidden hyphenated meaning in Be-eena, though I am sure the critic will suck the book dry and author-interpret Beena. Yes, yes, I have my reasons for choosing the name. Have patience. Your eyes crackle like hers. You have eyes like her, my Guruji. Green, and slashing like a machete. "If you bring a gun into the story, in the end, it must go off," she says. That's when I get mad at you, *Readerji*. I am no large-lapped goddess, churning out word after word, which you devour, chug, chug, left, right, until the book finishes. Can't you pull the trigger sometimes? And let me warn you there is no guru in the story either. I see, you want to co-create by including a police station in the story. How odd you want police in the story. Ah, because you don't trust my disorder. *Abra Kadabra Jadhu Manter Phoosh*, kiss a toad! And a one and two and a three sugars in my tea! Presto! There *is* an RCMP in this story but Indian *ishtyle*.

What do you mean, also a Petro-Canada gas station? *Readerji*, in a bullock village? Ah, you are only kidding! Ha! Ha! Ha! Finally, *Readerji* my *yaar*, you are de-starching but don't lose all your solemnity, what will happen to Beena?

I am not allowing you to read? I am chaotic, an interrupter, untrustworthy, fibber. Whoa! Whoa! I will tell you two things, and then I will disappear, in a flick second.

Beena's village has a *panchayat*. *Panch* means five. Five fingers. Five wise men of the village who handle disputes and maintain law and order. Oh yes, *Readerji*, Beena's father, Pindi, is one of the *panchayat-wallah's*. Hey, you know Pindi! So, your critic thinks Pindi is a scholar? *Readerji*, forget the critic with the small "c." Come with me a little farther. There are many hearts in Beena, yes, Pindi's included.

And now finally, *Readerji*. Turn around, it is time. Your hand. This is the edge of Beena's village. No, I still cannot abandon you. First, pour some water in the bathing bucket. Beena's mother is fanatic about cleanliness. Once you are through, rub the bucket well with sand and rinse it thoroughly. It should gleam like Mr. Sunlight's bulge. Yes, yes, I know this is in poor taste. But not the time to argue, my pet. It is hot *Readerji*, so why don't you bathe under the *pipal* tree?

. . . Tepid water. The water splashing on the baked sands sprouts peppery smells. There is a sudden gust of wind and the air is hued with the smell of mangoes. And then, thud, a mango falls.

"*Amma*, let me go, a mango's fallen."

"It won't run away, let me finish your hair."

"*Amma*, gently!" Beena's slender form is caught between her mother's strong legs.

Beena's mother grunts an acknowledgement. Under her rough fingers, the saucer of coconut oil clatters.

"Don't hunch child, how can I do your scalp properly?"

Beena has a heavy wave like a squirrel's tail and in sunlight, her black hair glints purple. When her mother is lost in thought, her fingers turn violent in her hair.

When Beena is a child, her mother makes a bony basin with her thin legs and sinks her into it. Hoarsely, she sings:

Sleep child sleep!
Harass not your mother
who has
yet to boil the *dal*
and grind spices.
Lie soft
so I can fetch water.
The floor is unswept
and Baba's trousers unpatched.
Child,
I have forgotten about firewood
yet yet yet
Oh scuttle off to sleep!

Beena also remembers her mother's ringed finger. She no longer wears the ring. She asks her about the ring but her mother's eyes only fill up. Beena cannot bear when her mother cries. She can't remember the ring except for the rhythmic thick sounds it made on her forehead, when she lay in her mother's lap, as a child. Each time her mother's hand came down on her forehead, her face must have screwed up like now, two wiry slits with thorny lashes. A dreadful gray creeps over her crunched face.

"Beena!, why do you always jump like that? You make my heart fall out! Up! Your hair is done."

I am Beena's mother. As a young bride, when I stand in the doorway of my husband's home, everyone gasps, even the village priest, who is supposed to be above such matters, for my colouring is that of limpid gold. Even now, with Beena shot up, the priest says it outright to our shopkeeper, "*Lalaji*, how can you say this clotty honey is pure? In this village we know that the clearest honey must measure up to Pindi's wife's colouring." The market crowd laughs. *Lalaji* does not let the *pandit* get away. "*Panditji*, don't stick me with a wandering bowl in my prime. How can I explain to your milk-lined stomach that dirty juice oils commerce?"

I have left my ring in *Lalaji's* care. Until Beena's wedding. It is a powerful ring with three rubies and two sapphires. Will hold merit amidst her shoddy dowry. There is also a silver water pot. Beena's father — I cannot leave anything to him. My shoulders are heavy. So heavy.

Yes, I am Pindi's wife.

I fell in love with my husband's walk. Tight gait of hips and hair flying back. There is a song in my village, "whenever the city-boy walks like this, the virgin's heart is fish out of water." Even now he startles me. The blue sky falls back as he strides forward, diminishing the mango tree and the thatched huts. His bent hip swerves, just, just so. It rushes his beauty and my green bangles turn dark.

That hot sleepy afternoon by the well. Shabnam and I are eating raw mangoes. Our skirts hitched up for any breeze. Now I am called Beena's mother. Pindi's wife. But my name is Dhano.

"Dhano, look, a city goat released our way. *Ooi*, he is wearing gold eye glasses, like white *dipti afficer*."

"Shabnam, pull down your skirt! His vision with four eyes must be sharp."

"*Ooi Babuji*, you with four eyes, in our village, the well is woman-space. You walk over here informally. Why? Is my friend Dhano getting married to you?"

"*Babuji*, my friend is cocky. Are you lost?"

"Perhaps I am. *Bibiji*, you with the edged tongue, tell your friend that her colour is intoxicating as a dimple.

"*Babuji*, so this is how city-men praise women, with a saki-wine tongue?"

"Forgive my indelicate comparison. Your Dhanoji's colouring is warm like butter and honey."

"Easy city-*Babuji*, you may slip on your oily-tongue, and this would be a pity, because your city strut has knocked us senseless. But really *Babuji*, our Dhano isn't a Maharani of some bakery. Butter and honey, hah!"

"Don't you offer a visitor water, friend of Dhano?"

"In our village, to feed you water, stranger-*Babu* is half the ritual."

"The other half?"

"Marriage *dholaks*, city-*Babu*."

"*Babuji*, I apologise for Shabnam's insolence."

"Dhanoji! Thank you for intervening. Your friend's tongue is nothing like shabnam-dew. It's lightning sharp. Will you pour water for me? I may receive some sweetness from your bounty."

"*Ooi Babuji* with four eyes, careful you don't get cramps in your tongue."

"Shabnamji, tell your friend I will seal the vacant half of the ritual with *dholaks* and feed her a tumbler of almond milk."

He kneels by me and holds out cupped palms. I lift my silver water-pot in one big arc and pour out a waterfall. He catches my eyes in an eye-lock.

"My name is Pindi," he says.

Readerji, Beena's father, Pindi. Yes, I am back. Pindi is a scholar. Actor. Actually, neither. His speech is slightly chilled at the top. Scholars and actors cultivate the brisk tone. Never fails to harness an audience. (Even your critic.) Pindi the village hero.

I can't resist to deviate, *Readerji*. "Hero" is a "ping" word for me. Oh no, in Beena's story, there are no heroes. But for a while, pretend there is a young widow. (Really, I can't resist this deviation.) It's like a *pucca*-ripe film script.

Story (and *Ooi Readerji*, see this through a lens): There is a young widow. Her husband is butchered on the train. It is 1947. Partition of India. The husband and wife have left everything and are fleeing to India on a ghost train from Lahore. But her husband is butchered on the train. The hero of our story is a *Teacherji*. The refugee widow makes her new home in his village, the village where the train drops off all the refugees from Pakistan. This *Teacherji* is a radical. He wants change after independence. With the British ousted, it is now the turn of the Brahmin rule-setters. Away with the practice of wife burning on her husband's pyre. Away with widow exile and her food without garlic. Shake life into her mummy existence. Let the red marriage vermilion seep into her bloodless hair parting. Let her wear passionate green bangles.

Of course not *Readerji*, this is not a teacher-student romance, leave that to the Harlequin caste. But it is a teacher and widow romance. *Yaar*, we are talking progress. Feminism.

(Action): The radical *Teacherji* blocks her path. She is returning from the river. He asks her for water from a widow's pot! In her confusion, the white-clad widow, with loose blowing hair tilts her pot and fills his cupped palms. *Fatafat* the Panchayat gathers under the banyan tree.

O the commotion *Readerji!*

Heaved dust, hooves, children thrown up their mothers' waists, clanking of padlocks on shops, men's voices thrown right across, only to be drowned by temple bells, and picnic food.

Oh yes, *Readerji*, picnic food is a must when stripping takes place. Who wrote that story, you know, after witnessing a violent beating, the heroine says she could eat a horse? This is no theft or shopkeeper fight-commotion. *Yaar*, a widow has stepped out of bounds. Hero-*Teacherji* will get a beating. But it is the widow's end. She should have known better.

Deftly, the hawkers form an unending line, with baskets full of roasted peanuts, spiced peas, fried cassava dipped in paprika, coconut cubes, and sweet creamy *burfi* spotted with purple flies, but no one cares. The widow has already created a juicy hunger. Food and picnic. Blaring loudspeaker churns out fast-fast songs.

Readerji, ping! I tell you, I can see this all on the screen. The middle part: their eye love story and how it all began (*Ooi*, I've yet to work out the details). But right now, I want to run to the end. The Brahmin-Khomenis wait with *lathis* and stones to hurl at our avant-garde hero. His forehead gleams and the cool green veins mapping his temples burst with power. He turns toward the widow, his last look, deep as a tongue in the desert (rub that frown of yours! I think the image conjures urgency/passion. So what if it doesn't make sense. Don't be such a tight accountant). His last look is really a tongue kiss (you cannot kiss on the Indian screen but all professional cinema goers know that deep-deep look is *really a kiss*). The hero is about to open the door, ready to be kicked in the face and belly.

But the widow hurls him round (their first touch and in the background the *dholak* goes wild! *dha-dhin dhin dhin*). She picks a blade which he uses for sharpening pencils from his desk and makes a gash in his thumb. Clutching his bloody thumb, she paints her hair parting. Now she is married to him. Her hair parting a pumping red. She pushes him behind her and opens the door. She steps out. He follows. (Cut.)

I am Pindi, the tailor. Never wanted to be a tailor but somehow I have become one. I live for my newspaper from the United Kingdom. It is greatly revered by the villagers because it is from *Vilayat*, the land of my British sahibs, my mother and father. The villagers insist that all sahibs live in *Vilayat*, London country. I tell them about America but they are not interested. The postmaster treats the paper reverently. Before my house he stops at Shiva's temple. The *Vilayat* paper under his arm. No one will steal it from his government khaki letter carrier, but it is out of respect for the newspaper. That's why my paper arrives tied with marigolds and a yellow speckle of food at the top. The Postman's offerings at the temple returned after being blessed by the priest. Yes, the villagers never tire of feeling the newspaper. When the postmaster arrives, Beena's mother brings my tea, never in a tumbler but a proper cup and saucer. I like to frown and let my chin sink into my chest as I scan the headlines. The postmaster withdraws silently. I have never been to *Vilayat*. I know I never will. I label all garments sewn by me: "By Pindi of Jamuna Village, London Returned."

Readerji, in the evenings, everyone gathers around the Banyan tree to listen to Pindi. He adjusts his gold glasses and relates to the villagers the real news. "Real news is from *Vilayat*," he tells them. His fringed shawl never slips off his shoulder. " 'One step for Man and a giant step for Mankind' says Neil Armstrong, the first man to set foot on the moon."

A village boy asks, "Pindi *Baba*, the *Vilayat*-London sahibs have even reached up there! They are God's special chosen, no?"

"Child, how many times must I tell you that *Neil-Babuji* is from America."

"But *Baba*, even Amrika is in London country, no?"

The village Granny who is a medicine mother and the keeper of stories pushes Pindi's shawled shoulder, "*Ooi* Pindi child, what fairy wonder have your white *Babus* done now?"

Pindi laughs. "Granny of the village, first of all, they will give your story of *Mamaji* who lives on the moon an eternal holiday! Grannyji, such stories you make of a wife's brother living on the moon. And when the moon looks scratched, it means *Mamaji* is carrying sticks on his back, and when the moon is low and swift between puffy dark clouds, *Mamaji* is playing 'shut your eyes' with the children."

"O villagers, and when children want to hear stories, don't send them to me but to Pindi, the favourite child of sahib *Babus*. Hah, as if the children will be content with stories of stiff machines on *Mamaji's* moon!"

Everyone giggles but they look at Pindi widely. He knows so much. *Readerji*, Pindi even swayed your intelligent critic.

> At one time Beena's mother had soft eyes. Now I could stitch up her taunting eyes and chop off Beena's curving hair. Shabnam's lightning would have matched my passion. But I fell in love with my wife's colouring. Like honey, like bread gathering gold in warmth.

Beena catches her mother's sharp glare at her father as soon as he steps into the courtyard. Beena rushes to her father to deviate his attention. "Come *Baba*, wash your hands, I will set out the food."

Beena's mother storms into the kitchen to join her daughter. "Why is he home for lunch today? Is he unwell?"

"He had to go to post office to fill out a money order to send to the landlord. The landlord will remain in the city for another month."

"Is he planning to open shop this afternoon? Or is he going to spend the afternoon with his *Vilayat* papers. Those papers are my husband's other wife, and my wretched enemy."

"*Amma*, let *Baba* eat in peace."

"Let him have peace. That's his male-tribe right. Worrying about my daughter's dowry is all my headache. What's it to this village if the *Vilayat* country catches fire? Can't your father stick his nose in his own kitchen for once?" She grabs the straw hand fan, sprinkles water on it, and goes into the courtyard. She fans her husband while he eats.

"When I prepared the tiffin for you this morning, you never mentioned that you were coming home in the peak of the afternoon."

"To visit the Post Office was not an item in my plans. My good friend Mirza Rashid and I entered into a discussion, and in the midst of our discourse, the matter of rent occurred to me and so I repaired to the Post Office."

> Yes husband. Revel in philosophies. Sit with your cronies, you empty spoon of the white sahibs. You would even praise the white sahibs' drawstrings! Let Beena age unbrided. Even in this frightening burden, I cannot ask your shoulder.

"I made my way to Ram Lal, the book seller next door," continues Pindi, "and gave him the food. His wife, as you well know, is away at her parents."

> Why husband, why? In the tiffin, I had packed a large coconut biscuit, an offering from the temple. No, not for *you!* My Beena loves these biscuits. I packed it out of wifely duty. Always, husband first. My true *dharma*. Damn!

"Beena, take this fan and sprinkle more water on it so your *Baba* can eat in cool peace. And Beena's father, won't you have more carrot *achar*, your daughter's favourite."

Nothing pleases my mother more than the arrival of the milk seller. She squats beside him in the courtyard, feet newly washed. She won't cook anything in milk. Fresh from the cow, a tumbler of milk is poured for my father and myself. She sings to me then:

One day
He will come
The king of grooms
Saffron turbaned, kohled eyes
And lift my Beena
Bathed in milk
She will rise from his navel
And encircle his shoulder
under the hood of
the unhurt Goddess
My Goddess of Protection

"*Hai* Beena, this silver-pot is your dowry piece! How dare you open the trunk!"

"*Amma*, I had nothing to do. It is such a heavy afternoon, not even a crow on the roof."

"Then come daughter, let me oil your scalp."

"And tell me the story of the silver water-pot."

"Once upon a time, by the well one day, on a hot, slumbering afternoon, two girls with hitched skirts laugh and eat raw mangoes. One of the girls has a honey-yellow skin, like the flesh of a chickpea. Her friend is bold, her tongue lightning. She sees the groom-prince first. I remember his stylish pyjamas and his brocade hip belt. His walk slicing the sluggish afternoon. . . ."

Beena gently removes her mother's fist from her hair. The greased fist heavy on Beena's shoulder.

"When he asked for water, he knelt by me and held out cupped hands. I lifted my silver pot in one big arc and poured out a waterfall. He said, 'My name is Pindi.' "

Beena is washing her hair. She takes a bunch of hair and throws it over, not caring when the wet strands smack her shoulder. Her back has flushed, spindly marks. She feels the clutch of coconut oil which sticks her hair together.

> *Amma*, drink from this waterfall pot. Throw back your head and let the water cool your ashed liver. Mother mine, you are a bride. Your thick ring glitters. You stand in the hushed doorway. And *Panditji* keeps staring at you. When you meet your husband's eye, he hues you pink. In his gaze, you stand under a pomegranate shower. Open your mouth wider, mother. I am your unhurt Goddess. Your Goddess of Protection.

No, not yet, she decides, and grabs more hair soap. She has her father's dreamy throat in her fingers. Her digging fingers tear into her scalp, and where the scratching is violent, the soap burns.

Beena's mouth waters.

Readerji, don't shout. All these stories knotted together are also giving me a headache. What? No *Readerji*, no one can be at our door. Listen, Beena is yours-mine. This is *our zenana*. Textbook stories of this equals that are a critic's formula. *Yaar-Readerji*, life isn't organized linearly because it is constantly piling. When I go to heat the milk or clean the fridge, other small things happen along the way: I pick up my mother's sock from the couch (which really needs to be cleaned), close the bathroom door, slam down the receiver when I realize it is a salesman, and finally, finally, I come to the milk. God, I hope the saucepan is clean. Similarly, a story is never linear. A story's collar bones are full of meat — by her very nature, she is massing constantly.

Indeed, what happens to Pindi? Both you and your critic are partial to him. *Yaar*, the satisfaction from this kind of fiction is you cannot compel a single intention or conclusion.

You are getting edgy *Readerji*, are you about to chop off my nose? Okay, let's talk about Pindi. Why are you staring at the door? What do you mean, Beena is outside?

Readerji, don't spook me. No, I don't hear her scraping her scalp. She does not exist outside the door. Of course I'm sure — I'm writing her! Because . . . enough! Look, I don't like your game. Come back! *Readerji*, NO!

Be a Doctor

There are no trees where we live. It is a new area. Cheap and so flat. No matter how far the bus is, you can see it straight. When I go in to get a glass of milk and come out again, it is still there, moving on and on. It isn't like this back home in Tanzania. First the bus dips and you can't see it, and when you see it, it has begun climbing, heaving upward, slower than a tortoise's tortoise. Sometimes, the men have to get out and push the bus. Once, a tourist lady in khaki trousers and pink sunglasses got out with the men to push the bus. The men didn't know what to say. They all bunched up to one side. Finally, an elderly mama rose and stepped out of the bus. She held out her hand to the tourist lady, who climbed back into the bus.

As soon as the climb is over, it is time for a party. No one comes on a bus without food. Bus food is special. Coca-Cola is always warm, and the cake smells of eggs. There is dried fish, cassava dipped in paprika water, and triangle *samosas* stuffed with mincemeat and peas. Then the bus-driver and the conductor do their ceremony, like hosts, when they cut mangoes and pass the slices around. I can't get used to their tender gestures. But they even do tough things tenderly. Opening the valves in the fat, snake-twirled tires with coaxing fingers. Their round mouths wet with spit.

Sometimes they are under the bus, their rubber slippers sticking out. We loiter about waiting for the bus to be fixed. The driver and the conductor always call each other nephew. They know just when to gather us into the bus before a herd of elephants suddenly appears out of nowhere. There is no haste. But the driver is already in the bus and the conductor's beckoning thump on the side of the bus is in rhythm with "*tembo, tembo*," the Kiswahili word for elephant. In the bus, we wait for the familiar waddle. A heavy swish like round *matkas* full of water and the swaying herd emerges. We can't see the calves, not yet. But when the herd crosses the road, we catch glimpses of the calves in the inner circle, between rocking flanks. The driver starts the bus after the herd disappears into the forest again.

The driver and the conductor don't care for time except when the women don't come out of the hotel washrooms after the allotted fifteen minutes. The conductor is mad when the women disobey but they always do. He swings his black purse full of shillings on his shoulder and bangs on the walls of the bus, with his fist. As if they can hear his noise in the hotel washrooms. The bus driver honks non-stop and yells, "Let them take all the time, the rhinos and elephants must also see them swagger beautiful." His remarks make the rest of us titter.

We buy everything from K-Mart. The Chinese shop here and us. Neither of us uses credit cards. Always cash. At Safeway though, Mum has started paying by cheque. She never bends low over the cheque. No wasted movement, then a tear and flick, the cheque is in the hands of the cashier. Father doesn't like it, paying by cheque, but Mum says this way she can control the budget better.

An Indian woman in an orange sari stands in front of Father in the K-Mart line. She carefully holds a frothy white blouse. The cashier's eyes are undented, huge blue. (Romaine's eyes are green, a wacky green. They keep changing colour. When she is bored, she rolls up her eyes to stare at her hair.) The cashier speaks slow and loud to the woman, like she is explaining to her something complicated. "This item is not on sale." The Chinese when they make a mistake, you can't tell. Their eyes don't change and they are quiet. The Indian woman twitches her hand, making her weighty gold bangles juggle. The hairs on her arms are quite dark. "*Haya*, I not understanding what you peoples write. Why blouse not for sale?"

Father begins to scan magazine headlines, his body turned, so that he stands a little out of line, as if to let the people in the line-up know that he is not with the woman in the orange sari. He has forgotten about me. His shoulders are rigid.

His clenched rage loosens in the parking lot, "If she can't read, can't she even dress decent? That tight blouse and then a flood of hanging stomach. Really, I tell you, we must improve our image!"

Father works at the Bay parking lot, and he wears sweaters that look too big on him. In a queue, everyone looks bigger than him. Back home, when he read *Time*, we didn't disturb him. He read knowledgeably and turned his head to one side when he coughed. We knew of *Maclean's* after we came to Canada. But *Time* is big in Tanzania. He doesn't buy the magazine here though; he reads it in the doctor's office. He is keen on flyers. "Dilshad," he calls Mum, "There is a special on Mazola this Saturday at Food City." Our basement is like a miniature grocery store. They often go down and switch on the special bulb that floods the basement and take stock of the items afresh: crates of tomatoes, fresh lemons, four kinds of mango pickle, lime pickle, two irons, basmati rice. Toilet rolls, sanitary napkins, and garbage bags almost cover an entire shelf, bulbs, Kenyan coffee, pop, tabasco, Mazola oil, a red kite with yellow speckles, spades, nutmeg, Pledge, green lentils, red lentils, blue window cleaners, china grass, Benares lace, four boxes of Tide, Chivas, curtain rods, hooks, *ghee*, two sets of hot hair rollers (neither Mum nor I use rollers), baking powder, winter tires, hoses, two emergency kits, and a bale of tough cotton (which Mum cuts in strips when she waxes her legs).

Saturdays are different in Tanzania. Every Saturday, we go on a picnic. Often to River Chekacheka, the laughing river. As soon as we climb out of the car, it starts laughing. Ha-ha-ha. Wyah-ha-ha-ha. We don't go on picnics alone. The Bhajajs, the De Souzas and the Patnas are with us too. We take three cars. All us kids clamber on the rocks, and join the river. Ha-ha-ha. Wyah-ha-ha until we get the hiccups. Then Mrs. Bhajaj brings us *nimbu*-lemon water. She says, "Enough, I have had enough of your crocodile belly torture. After *nimbu* water, you goats help unpack the hampers, *pronto fatafat*."

From Thursday onward, we beg Mrs. Bhajaj to take her large pumpkin so that all us kids can go with her. Mrs. Bhajaj calls us goats because we pester her. "Your goat-boat *Meeh, Meeh* and your butter-vutter flattery won't soften me," she tells us. We pay no heed. We lure her with delicacies: "I will press your feet," "I will fan you while you nap," "your *nimbu pani* won't lack ice." Natasha and Pinki De Souza phone Mrs. Bhajaj in the morning, and Mohammed Patna phones during mid-meal time, and I phone her in the evening. Only Raj and Renu Bhajaj are exempted from phoning and anyway they always end up in someone else's car. Mrs. Bhajaj is special. She isn't like Mummy or Mrs. Patna who remain in the kitchen when there are too many guests at a party. When Mrs. Bhajaj does the Twist, she wears black slacks. She wears a fringe just like Sadhana, the film actress. In her orange pumpkin, we sing Hindi film songs, especially the ones Sadhana sings in films. They have a fast beat:

> I'll love *khulam-khula* openly
> Taa-raa-rum-paa
> Won't hide
> Won't bide
> till *bahar*-spring
> Raj-Prince
> rum-paa, rum-paa
> this heart beats
> thump-aa, thump-aa
> *bekarar*-impatient
> Come on, come on

And we eat roasted peanuts. Mrs. Bhajaj tailgates lorries until they nervously let her pass but she doesn't leave them. She rolls down her window and yells at the driver, "What, have you sacrificed this road to your granny?" If the driver throws something abusive at her, she knocks his speech midway, "Yah, yah, and you socket yours in your wobbly granny's," and then swooshes off. We don't completely understand her build-up of words, but we know they are richly dirty, and are very excited. While driving, Mrs. Bhajaj never drapes her sari over her shoulder but tucks it into her waist. She has thin muscled ivory arms, and her blouses have a vast neckline. She has the loveliest blouses: one green like early corn, one mustard, and one pink like lipstick colour in *Style*.

One Saturday, after East Indian buildings, mills, and schools are nationalised, Mrs. Bhajaj drives slowly to River Chekacheka. We don't sing Hindi songs. Mohammed Patna no longer goes to school.

A tutor comes to his house. Pinki tries to tickle me but I pinch her stomach. Mrs. Bhajaj has the radio on. President Nyerere's speech is over and it is now the Comedy Hour. Leo Elvis is on. He used to be a singer at the Hotel Kilimanjaro but now he is Mandela Atebe.

> "These East Indians, I tell you, are strange. Who is their God? I ask you my brothers, my nephews, who is their God? A cow! They worship a cow! So what do you expect? This black servant, spindly like spider legs works for one woman. You know her? Oh my brothers, my nephews, you must know her!"

The audience laughs.

> "Ah, I see you have met her! Who is she? One fat Indian mama. She does nothing; nothing but fans herself. Her black servant cooks, he cleans, he washes, he dries, he shops, he digs — I mean he digs her garden, not in her of course! She is too good for him then!"

The audience roars.

> "Hey my friends, *cheka*, *cheka*, laugh for it is time to laugh and let me tell you a joke. So this servant one day says to this East Indian Queen Elizabeth of us Blacks, 'Mama, my legs are thin, thin like spider legs, I can't carry all these utensils on one tray.' So the fat darkie Royal Queen advises, 'First carry the tray in, and then fall all you want!' My brothers and nephews, this is the East Indian mentality. It is nobody's fault, we Africans have slave brains. First the British, Big Bwana and his gun and pipe. And then the East Indian money frog. . . ."

"That mother fucker . . . Nyerere's empty spoon, the crocodile flatterer," Mrs. Bhajaj says and switches off the radio. "Who gave Leo Elvis the warm shillings to go to America if not an Indian. No, this is not mentioned. And don't I send Cook Kwesi's son to the same school that my children go to? Nyerere wants to do things *ek dum fatafat* like there is no tomorrow. What does Nyerere want? That I wear grass skirts and skin lions in the Mikumi forest?" No one laughs. Then Mrs.

Bhajaj screeches on the brakes. Pinki jerks forward and gets stuck between the two front seats. Five policemen block the road. They are not carrying guns but *pangas*. One of them wears a baseball hat. There are no police vans on the side of the road. Only the uniformed men, spooky bright, out of nowhere. Their *pangas* aren't shiny but huge, the broad blades close to their shins. I have only seen *pangas* in museums before.

Mrs. Bhajaj doesn't bother with Pinki. She simply reverses, swivels the car around and drives back, honking wildly. We don't go for picnics after this.

"I want you to become a doctor. I want your name in lights," Mum tells me. I am not allowed to wear nail polish. If I watch any channel other than PBS, she asks, "Don't you have any homework to do?" or tells me to remove the garbage. She works as a secretary in a downtown insurance office. From her first pay cheque, she brought home a microwave. Every Saturday night, she cooks meals for six days. Father isn't allowed to help either. Sometimes, she allows him to make her a cup of tea. Father makes a proper tray with a tray cloth and tea in a porcelain pot, and then yells, "Dil . . . Di-lu!"

"Eat slowly. Your mouth will burn," she tells Father at the supper table. I know that when Father ate his food noisily in Tanzania, it pleased her. "Is it good?" she would ask, rubbing her hands on the chapatti cloth.

Father dresses like a hero in Tanzania. He wears khaki trousers and a mud green belt and safari boots. When they go out, he stands at the bottom of the stairs while Mum descends in a peacock blue sari.

His mud green belt is too big for him now. I have it. It hangs on a nail in my room.

Father screams in his sleep. In a booming voice, he screams at Juma, our houseboy, for not starching his shirt, and when he screams at President Nyerere, his voice breaks; he rasps, "Nyerere, I will kill you . . . I will rape your mother . . . you dog fucker," and Mum holds him, murmuring powder words like prayers. When Father has a bad dream, I am allowed to sleep with them. Once he screams so loudly, my stomach aches. In the morning, I have my period.

After the swearing ceremony, we sing "O Canada." I feel silly singing it, like I feel silly singing Christmas carols with Romaine. Romaine has shiny hair at the top but full of split ends at the bottom.

Once she takes me to a Salvation Army store and we buy second-hand trousers. Father and Mum gasp and Romaine looks so sorry. Mum says, "Never mind," but Romaine is still miserable. Mum says to her, "Romaine, come with me to the bathroom." She chops off her split ends. Then Romaine wants bangs but Mum does not know what she means. They call me. I tell Mum that Romaine wants a fringe.

The man beside me has his hair falling in his eye but he doesn't care. He sings "O Canada" deep and vibrating. He is nuts about Canada. I roll up my eyes like Romaine.

After the ceremony, Mum hugs me and says, "You will be a doctor." She doesn't say it hard. She says it toy-soft. She sees nothing. I don't want to be a doctor. I want to be Romaine.

We are on her Grandparents' farm. Though she does not have a licence, she is allowed to drive on the farm. The sky is full of ice-cream colours. Romaine has run out of windshield fluid. She uses snow. We rush through the flat road, and it opens wider and wider. I feel snug. She turns to me, and asks, "Want to drive?"

Aisha

I can smell the milkman's smell. It is like no other smell. I can smell it more sharply than the jasmine bush growing by our well, more sharply than the red perfumed oil Grandmother uses on my woolly hair, so that it becomes smooth and straight, almost like a long-haired broom. His stink isn't a killer stink — nothing like brown-green froth oozing out of soggy body cells, once packed and salute-upright. In the milkman's smell, there is the thin, sweetish persistence of fresh dung and the sour-clean gust of a baby's vomit. I know its shape too. It isn't straight like a margin line but puffy because wherever he goes, his smell grows and bulges like yeast. The milkman's long *kanzu* is clean, always white and starched. I relish in calling his strange smell a panty smell, although only secretly. I am good at secrets.

"Aisha!" Grandmother calls from the verandah, "Fetch the milk saucepan, and is Juma in the kitchen?"

I find Juma in the kitchen but he is twitching his shoulders and wildly shaking his head at me. I laugh because he looks like a jittery monkey.

Grandmother hears me laughing because she shouts, "Ju-u-u-ma! Two teas and make it *chapa chapa*!"

Grandmother is very beautiful and her shout isn't a needle shout that pierces your eardrum. It has small waves but her words have a talon's grip. Juma knows that. He flies to the kitchen door, "*Ooi* Mama, at once Mama!"

But in the kitchen, it is different. "Whenever that udder squeezer is here, everything must be *chapa chapa*," Juma says, as he thrusts the freshly emptied batter bowl under a furious gush of hot water. "I tell you, am I some office machine? Slip in an order and out it comes at the end." He is making savoury cassava fritters. I greedily inhale the smells of coriander, chilies and peppers that emerge from the steam.

"You Aisha, get away from the sink before you melt your nose."

I jump away. My nose is as flat as a boxer's.

I set the saucepan by the milk urn in the verandah. Grandmother pours tea in tiny pale cups. The milkman holds the cup handle with his first two fingers and thumb. His little finger remains softly curved. He wears a silver signet on his little finger. He isn't like the milkmen in tattered shorts at the market place — no rough Adam's apple or raspy tufts of hair on broad knuckles.

Each time he comes to the mansion, I stare solid at his armpits but they are fastidiously white as the rest of his robe. And his toe nails in rope sandals gleam. But his smell is always there. The puffy panty smell.

Grandmother and the milkman don't talk much while having tea. They share a silence that isn't heavy like mosque silence. It is an airy silence which allows everything to enter: the steady beat of Juma's pestle, the hot smell of ironed clothes, sudden laughter from the street, a honk. Sometimes the milkman sighs or Grandmother will get up to water the roses. Otherwise, they sit and watch the sky turn pink, and heavier and heavier pink, until the sky storms red, and the palm leaves make little sways in the falling sunset wind. Evenings are Grandmother's and the milkman's. But I am scared of evenings. They are secretive and watch with invisible undented eyes. (I never walk under trees in the evenings because ghosts are up there praying.) In postcards, evenings don't come out spooky soft like they really are.

When the milkman places the saucepan full of milk by Grandmother, her face becomes a mass of unmanageable softness as if it will ripple outside her face. She is never like this with me. With me, her oval nostrils flare, and she clamps on her smile and she clamps off her smile.

"When is Mummy returning home?" I ask Grandmother, although I am not interested in Mummy's return. The milkman has gone but her face is still soft.

"In a fortnight."

I can still smell the milkman. I am sitting in his chair.

"You and the milkman, I mean *Mzee* Mamudu, you don't talk much. You watch palm trees."

"Strange what children notice. Do we?"

"All the time. And Juma doesn't like him."

"Of course, Juma is our Queen Elizabeth."

Before what happened, Juma did as he pleased. Spending time at the Tusker Sambarero bar when it was past tea time or baking himself a cake, pink icing and all. He kept the mansion keys, even the key that unlocks Grandmother's steel cupboard, where she keeps the passports and chunks of notes held by fat elastic bands (Grandmother even has under the table British money in her steel cupboard). But after that evening, Grandmother has taken over, becoming a giant eagle, and Juma goes all shaking dumb before her.

Grandmother tells me that Juma returned to his village because he was very sick. A lie.

Her face is still full of ripples. Their miserable teas.

"Why can't Juma keep the mansion keys anymore? Is he still sick?"

"Not anymore. Coming back to no grand keys, no nothing has cleared him of his heady freedom."

"Then he isn't bad, like in stealing, you mean?"

"He just became to big for his boo . . . hey you, what's the matter with you?" Now all her ripples have gone, "So young, and already you have your Mother's talent for question on top of question. Rip off all the skin and thrust out everything open naked. Why should you care? Let the world gape!"

Whenever Grandmother gets mad at me, she brings in Mummy. I don't say anything. I put on my dead expression and let my eyes drop low on my cheeks as if I am sleeping, and no one can get to me. Not Grandmother, nor people like Mr. Jeevan, who asks me dead centre in the market-place, even when Mummy is in town, "Now where is that painter Mother of yours?" as if Mummy does nothing important. Maybe if she were a doctor, it wouldn't be so bad. At least then Mr. Jeevan would call her *Lady Doctor-ji*, full of respect. With my dead face, I forget who is standing in front of me, Mr. Jeevan or anybody. I have killed all her ripples.

Mummy's famous painting is at the *Uhuru* Gallery. The name *Uhuru* is very famous these days. If a pregnant woman is asked what she will name her baby if it is a son, she says *Uhuru*. The *brinjal-walli* told Grandmother that she was going to name her daughter Uhuria, and Grandmother's nostrils flared sleekly, "*Uhuru*, we know means freedom, but this Uhuria, pray tell us what that means?" The *brinjal-walli* said nothing but only rearranged her brinjals defiantly. Grandmother bought her brinjals but she hadn't finished with her. "With this *Uhuru* craze piling like an overflowing river, all face of Kiswahili will change. And then the British will have something to really laugh about, a belly full of hyena laughter. We can't even manage our language now that they have left."

Mummy got a medal for her painting from President Nyerere. She took me to Dar es Salaam to see it hanging at the *Uhuru* Gallery. When I saw the painting, I thought it was funny. The title didn't match the painting at all. Or as Juma would say, the title was ways-a-way in China. It was titled *Zebra Tanzania*, only there weren't any zebras in the painting, but two Dodoma women in *kangas* with tribal blue scars on their cheeks. They were pounding maize and wearing sunglasses!

"Is this a cartoon-like painting?"

"No . . . gosh no! Aisha, it is an allegory. See, can a zebra remain a zebra without having both the black and white stripes?"

"I don't think so."

"Right . . . what I want to show in this painting is that because Tanzania has got its independence, it must not refuse European help. In order to advance, we must not shun — say no to European advancements, like, like giant farm machinery which we can't make as yet, and there is no shame in adopting their comforts, like sunglasses these two tribal women are wearing. God knows, we need sunglasses in the Dodoma sun. See Aisha, Europeans, they are the white stripes in the painting who can help us, and they are part of us in some ways. And we Tanzanians must always, always retain our own stories . . . our culture . . . our own stripes."

"Black stripes."

"Yes. Now, do you understand?"

"A little, but not really. But I like your painting. I like funny paintings."

I am proud of Mummy and to the newcomers at school, the first thing at recess, before I buy Coke and peanuts or anything, I tell them right away that presidents like Kennedy and Tito visit *Uhuru* in Dar es Salaam where my Mother's painting hangs. This way they forget to give me that strange look because of my woolly hair and flat-wide nose.

It doesn't matter to me if Mummy is not like other mothers, with their hair scooped in greasy buns, cooking and cleaning all day long. The only time I feel like crying is when I see the women so proud, in starched saris and smelling of talcum power, strolling with their husbands in the evenings, passing Ramson's Cinema and Mr. Jeevan's Piccadilly Household and Sundries. Then I too wish Papa were alive — he would lift me high in the air, and I would shriek, "Papa, not so high, my panty will show!" And that Mummy didn't paint nor wear her awful bush shoes.

Now I know that Papa isn't dead. He ran away. I have never seen him. When I didn't know about Papa, I would run to Juma in the kitchen and ask, "Why did Allah take Papa?" and Juma would first give me tea with six teaspoons of sugar.

"*Weh* Aisha, stop talking ways-a-way in China. Child, if I was the Beneficent and the Merciful One, first things first, I would give you a white skin. Secondly, I would padlock Mr. Jeevan's penis-long tongue."

"Penisssss long tongue," I repeat.

"Aisha, stop that, or I will redden your mouth with chilies."

"White like Grandmother's skin?"

"Hey, I can do much better than her sallow skin, sagging like a cow's throat."

"Grandmother's skin is beautiful! Pale and yellow like peeled almonds."

"Well Aisha, yours I tell you, yours would be tip-top white, topper than European quality. I say, you will have to sit under an umbrella even in the evenings."

More than Grandmother's silent teas with the milkman, I hate Papa.

Mummy stroked my beady plait and said, "No need to miss Papa, darling. You have me, Aisha, my hope, exactly like I named you," and

I cried more, not because I missed Papa, but because Mummy's sobs came out hard and tight, as if her ribs were cracking.

But now, whenever Mummy is in town, I get out my doll from the bottom of the drawer, and show it to her.

"Queenie is so *gori-white*, like European, and her hair is soft as Benares silk."

Little spit forms at the corner of her mouth and her eyes are thick with water. Mummy cries easily. She isn't like Grandmother. I have never seen her cry. Mummy shouts at Grandmother.

"You don't respect the texture of Aisha's hair, forever coiling her hair! And now this white doll again, didn't I tell you to get rid of it?"

"You be Jesus to the Africans, my dear, save them. Aisha is in my care. And you Aisha, put the doll away. Have you no salt in your head, playing with dolls at your age?"

Mummy likes to do nice things for Africans. I wonder if she would have helped Juma? She was in Paris then.

Before, Juma was always laughing at Mummy, "She is always rushing as if to catch a slippery bus," because right when lunch was served, Mummy often jumped from her chair and shut the studio door and painted for hours. And sometimes, he crept into her studio to have a soaking belly laugh. And when a drawing cracked him up, he slapped his thigh, "Mother of mine, I wouldn't be caught with that one," pointing at a woman with an enormous stomach on her left side.

Not now. "*Weh* Aisha, I know you, now what game are you flagging, remembering the white doll only when your Mother is here?"

I put on my dead face.

And I refuse to go with her to the Lion Sher Singh Hotel, where all the truck drivers make a stop. When I was younger, at midnight, she whisked me in my pajamas and knotty hair to eat *muskaki* at the Lion Sher Singh Hotel. No one looked directly but I knew they were laughing at us, especially at Mummy, only she didn't know. She liked to eat the *muskaki* like the truck drivers, sliding the beef chunk off the skewer with her teeth, and when the peppered tamarind chutney got too hot, she opened her mouth to suck the air, and raised her hand high for cold water.

"Can't you paint simple flowers in a trough?" I ask her.

"Oh Aisha, how can you say that? Anyone can do that."

"Well, can't you wear heeled shoes at least?"

With Juma, if I see him on the kitchen steps, looking far, far away, it is easy for me to sit by him. I know it is *her* he is thinking about. The milkman's daughter. Juma's angel.

"I saw you two together, always at the Tusker Sambarero Bar. You sat by the far window, and she kept rolling the bottom of the window curtain until the top looked like a fluffed mosquito net."

He says nothing.

"They married her off quick."

He says nothing again, and then starts singing:

Yes angel, *nakupenda* my angel
But I have not a vessel, no *pesa*
I am defeated
Yes angel, *nakupenda* my angel

When Juma sings the "*nakupenda* my angel," the "I love you" part, it doesn't come out rough, grinding the coils of his throat. This is the best part of the song when everyone shrieks and whistles like mad. Juma sings without noise.

The milkman and his wife came to invite Grandmother, personally. His wife sat on the floor by Grandmother, who sat on the sofa, and the milkman grabbed my arms. It was the first time he touched me, and said, "You too, Granddaughter of the mansion." I smelt my fingernails later, they reeked of him.

Of course we didn't attend the wedding. They hadn't expected us to. But Grandmother sent angel a gold necklace set in red stones.

Two days before the wedding, Juma was in prison.

That whole day he sat on the kitchen steps drinking *pombe* and picking at this teeth. He didn't bother to hide the bottles, even from Grandmother. Just to see, I made several excuses to go into the kitchen. He wasn't the same Juma who cut sugar-cane in tiny rectangles and wrapped my text books in brown paper. The bottles sat on the cutting table beside the brinjals and the unwashed rice; huge bottles containing watery fuzzy stuff. Only once Grandmother passed his way. She placed a plate of cashew nuts and some fried potatoes by his side. "To fort your system against that sweet water," she said, pointing to the *pombe*. Juma didn't even look at her!

But that evening Juma went crazy. He staggered toward the milkman with tea slopping out of a chipped cup. "I will make it five goats," he told the milkman, but held out only four fingers. He was grinning away. The milkman smiled at Grandmother and his gold tooth was visible. Grandmother said nothing but her nostrils flared and her nose ring glinted. Both looked so high and separate from Juma. I was ashamed of Juma, and I hoped that Papa didn't have such white teeth in a black, sweaty face like Juma's.

"Aisha, go off and play. I will send for you, no, not the kitchen, play elsewhere," Grandmother commanded.

I went to my room and I didn't know when the milkman left. But I opened my door when I heard deep coughing. Juma was crying. Sometimes I couldn't hear what he was saying because he was hicupping. Grandmother's voice was usual with little waves, like she was buying chicken, or talking to Juma about a guest list.

"Marry someone from your tribe, and I will pay the bride price."

"Mama, I want to marry her. I know she is above me, but times have changed."

"Don't mouth freedom and *Uhuru* at me — and you have enough to pay for the bride price?"

"Mama, please Mama. I am close to reaching the bride price. I have two bales of cloth, a basket of grain, thousand shillings, and two goats."

"Your slippery fingers must have taken rest in my cupboard then . . . you were promising *Mzee* Mamudu five goats on the verandah?"

"You are my Mother and Father, Mama. I have grown up here. With your help . . . Mama, you must help me."

"*We* wouldn't." Grandmother is using the royal "We." The proper way to address servants. My chest hurts like it did when I fell from the mango tree in our *shamba*. I don't want Juma to be punished. One day, a new cloth-washer stole a tin of peanuts from the pantry, and Grandmother made him stick his finger in his mouth until it came out, mottled, moist blobs of chewed peanuts.

"We all have proper positions to maintain in life. Juma, marry someone from your own clan."

"Mama, times have changed."

"My ears are over-ripe with this freedom heat."

"But Mama, I beg you with a man's tears — don't do me so much dishonour, Mama, angel Mama. . . ."

"*Ooof*, you make so much tin noise!"

"Mama, reconsider. With Aisha's Mother, you had to. . . ."

"Why you pig's semen! I will have you locked up for lifting your filth-slick tongue on *Our* honour."

"You can't do nothing. Mama, isn't Aisha proof enough, and this is as best a proof as you can get, the holy mixture, straight from Allah."

"You will pay for this! All this lion noise because your black cocks can't remain idle for long. Be it yours or that black father of Aisha's who ran away, fresh after seeding my daughter."

"Mama, I beg of you. . . ."

"Yours won't remain idle for too long. Go away for a few days."

"You are my Mother and my Father, and I take all your insult. But I will marry angel. You can't stop me."

"I couldn't stop Aisha's Mother but your *Uhuru* I can stop, as easily as tripping a dog. One phone call, that's all."

That evening, I knew the truth, that Papa wasn't dead at all. All this while, I thought of him as having frothy white wings, like Christian angels. But my father lives and is blacker than Juma.

Juma returned after the short rains. Now he looks smaller. He still eats three platefuls of *ugali* and spinach red-bean curry for lunch. There are purple scars on his back.

When he returned, he had jaundice and Grandmother nursed him. She ordered new blankets for him from Piccadilly Household and Sundries, and lay crisp pajamas on his bed each night. She fed him boiled chick-peas and sugar cane juice. But once he recovered, Juma no longer had the keys. Grandmother wears them now, on her waist, and if he wants anything from the cupboard, Grandmother asks, "why do you want sugar — for a cake or for your own cup of tea?" Juma puts six teaspoons of sugar in his tea.

"*Whe-e-y* Aisha, *chapa chapa* girl, bring the milk into the kitchen," Juma calls out, "and why do you always linger when the milkman cushions here in the evening, you have no homework to do?"

"Finished."

"And the long, long face. You have friends ways-a-way in China or what?"

"Mummy is coming."

"Oh yes, then all time loses hands. That Mother of yours can make time go dizzy."

"You don't laugh at her anymore."

"Oh, I laugh all right. But I don't laugh with all my teeth. *Uhuru*, that's one mother fucker — it fucked me up, and it fucked up your Mother."

"I want to see Mummy's and Papa's wedding photos."

"Your Mother lost them in a flood."

"What flood?"

"I am still deciding. She has been in many floods."

I say nothing. Then I ask, "Mummy was in Paris when it happened but she must know."

"*Aye*, but when you get burnt drinking milk, then you blow and blow before you sip buttermilk."

"Juma, do you know where *she* lives?" (I am too shy to say angel in front of him.)

"She must be happy, because she didn't come, not once, even when I took care of everything and bribed the guard."

I want to touch Juma but I ask, "Where is Grandmother?"

"Let her go to China, I don't care. You watch the milk, not with one hard eye, but both hard eyes. I am going to the *shamba* to get mangoes."

"Juma, no! Now is the time when ghosts come out to pray."

"And I thought it was their pissing time."

I stay close to him. The *shamba* is just behind the mansion. As usual, the grass is high. Juma cleans the top of doors and bulbs under the huge lamp shades but Grandmother never bothers to ask him to cut the grass. In the wet season, mosquitoes come inside, but Grandmother refuses to have the grass cut timely.

The sky is turning inky blue now. The branches of the palm

trees gleam black. The dark trees in the *shamba* grow out of mid-air because of the enormous length of the grass. Although they are silent, they seem to have huge watching eyes. The air is heavy with the smell of mangoes. Mangoes and something else. It is so familiar.

There are sounds coming from the grass now. I yank at Juma's back pocket. He goes stiff, and I can feel the ghost's socket stare. I shut my eyes but jerk them open because Juma turns and clamps my mouth, almost squashing my nose, and then slowly he pushes me back but not before I see Grandmother's ivory shoulders and loose hair coming out of the tall grass. She is pushing against something.

The dreadful smell chokes my nostrils.

Paris in Bombay

Dear Uwe,

You could have held my hand tight that night. (After so many years, have I any claim to accuse you intimately?)

Or should I hurriedly tell you first that yes, I married Nikhil, and there is no difficulty of rupees, and our children have grown. And then slowly, ever so slowly, come to details like your beer and my sherry at Cafe Calabash. Is it still there? (Even now, my tongue swiftens after two sherries.) That small specked stone you got me from Kananaskis, its specks tough as dandelions. It is on my study desk. When I comb my newly washed hair or drape on a Benares sari, I bring it to my dressing stand.

The answer to your cautious, unasked question (oh yes, I can hear it) is, yes, I have kept at writing but remain startled when addressed as a writer. Even after a few (thin) books.

So yes, I have kept writing. Recognition? No Imam is after my kaffir head. Nor has my ink spilt so powerfully as to gather a fervid band of followers crying, "We succumb! We succumb!" (Do your blonde eyebrows still quiver when you ask a poking question?)

Ah, but I have fame. Recently, a critic from *The New Delhi Post* wrote, "Divya N. Raj's poetry reminds me of boiled cabbage and lukewarm ginger ale." There is this rough fame from *maha* critics and the truth is, in India, even cold ginger ale is dreadful.

Uwe, do you still count, starting from the thumb?—a little raise of the shoulder, hand close to chest, and then your thumb swings into action, "One." I watched you with an unfenced eye: your thin shoulders (still unironed shirts?) and hair delicate as gold dust on figurines. If you are smiling now, there is a slanting gash on your left cheek. When you laugh, it cuts your cheek in two. Forgive the cliché, but it is *special* when you laugh: two half cheeks and one whole cheek. My warmest *salaams* to you, my friend.

Some twitch or word or whatever . . . these spillings of yours, as I called them, turned into smells for me. They punched my head. Dazed, I watched them creep out of paper. One such smell, giddy and gymnastic, was *Paris in Bombay*.

Do you remember that rainy afternoon when we were in Riley Park, totally drenched and you decided to become an impressed Parisian? You stuck your arms sleek by your sides and your shoulders did a fluid sideways tilt, "*Oh la-la*," you said, and I, like a *bharat natyam* dancer, framed my head between my hands and rocked it sideways to the pattering chatter of the rain. And where trees formed a bunchy blanket, blocking its incessant chatter, the sound of rain turned into a swollen "sh." A sloshed walk with you, and *Paris in Bombay*. (It is a noisy story.)

What if one day, you come across the book? No, not at the library, where the stacked books look lifeless with so much waiting. I see *Paris in Bombay* open on your knee. You are in your office, which is circular (like the old one at University of Calgary), and the shelves bulge with clambering books. On your desk is a steel bucket filled with things, from filament tape to a bread knife. (You brought me flowers from the mountains once . . . thin powdery purple flowers.) As always, your swimming trunks (they were red then) are hung to dry at the back of your chair.

What would you do? Read the noisy novel with unbreathing silence . . . or thumb through it bewildered by so much worship? Like Heer's worship. But then I have not been acutely single to you like Heer was to her Ranjha. When Heer set out to search for Ranjha, who was banished to the desert, so blaring was her search for her beloved that God shook and descended to rescue her — only she said to Him, "but you are not Ranjha."

Whilst autographing copies at the Tagore Bookstore when *Paris in Bombay* first came out, I craned my neck, searching for you in the queue. I knew you would not be there. But I liked to imagine you there, tall and your clothes battered as ever, whilst I, the heroine, had on a chapeau, so black and swivel, shadowing my eyes.

Or as you thumb through the book, you notice a slight protrusion, and turning to the page (I have fifty-nine in mind for no reason, mon ami) you come across a pair of long feather earrings. Extravagant, that other world, that's where I am with you.

With Nikhil, I am not so giddy. I take inventory of what has to be starched, fetched, and fastened. I call this cornflakes-vinegar reality. I make stories from it now.

And yet, Nikhil is vivid as collar bones: deep and smooth with a steady pulse beating above. He resides in me like the lines of the dressing table he built for me. An oval mirror swings out of an oval frame and the rosewood neck gives way to a flat horizontal top for my comb and kohl. Then the piece continues downward, smooth and singular until it merges into its tortoise-humped base.

"*Writer-sahiba*," that's what Nikhil calls me, "after you close your study door for the day, come to me." (He is familiar to me as ancient vermilion.)

In your whirl, I might have lost my bangles and dusty gully. Uwe, there is an old Hindi song, "To live in your gully, To die in your gully." This gully is both my bond and anguish. It is only a *filmi* song but its anguish satisfying. The heroine's ash is warm between my fingers. (I have not seen the film. Never want to.) The song seeps this way and that in my own gully/landscape. Had I held out fingers hued in northern rosemary and thyme, you would have held my hand tight, only I would have never been able to wipe off their newness. (On my bridal palms, Nikhil's henna burnt a harvest orange.)

Does she still use green ink? I knew you got a letter every four days from Prince Edward Island. A dried stemless orange flower on the front of the envelope and she used green ink, always.

When we sat under the lamppost that night, my last night, you showed her to me. Not photographs, but drawings. On one page, her shoe with soggy laces, and on the facing page, her spread breasts. Your pencil followed her breath, tracing her flesh where it bulged and sank.

Why did you show her to me this truthfully? To jar what out of me, my friend?

Was she the one who came to you with rosemary and thyme? Still, you could have held my hand tight that night, because I have never let go of yours, as I can never let go of the space between my fingers.

In my study, where I write from four to sunrise, you are with me, swollen as a root, and in the vast bed and the cupboard full of his shirts and my kurta pyjamas, I am Nikhil smudged. (I apply his red *kum kum* between my breasts.)

What else? I never cried even when I got home, that night. But since then, I spill my hair (yes it is still long — the final "still" in this letter) over my breasts or cover them with a sheet. Just breasts, comfortable and lazy, remind me of her.

Divya

P.S. Sorry about the frayed edges of your *Paris in Bombay.* My first copy from the publisher. But I have slipped it into an envelope and removed it as many times. Perhaps today. And are you hastening to page fifty-nine?

The Play Begins

Readerji*, finally your eye has caught us, in the middle of this aisle, after feasting on the back of the woman in the ivory dress. Ah yes, the woman in the ivory dress has a banquet back, rotund. And same as you, *Readerji*, any gazer on her turns starer, can't get enough of her back — it is heady, like Madame Bovary's wine eyes, always leaving an unfinished starer/an unsatiated gazer.

The woman in the ivory dress has a saki back — languid and generous. But if you tilt your head sideways *Readerji*, candles glide up her back. Do you hear the peal of cathedral bells soaring out of her back? *Gazer-Readerji*, now her back slides down your eye, moist and tender and so heavy, as round coconut flesh.

In my story, there isn't a gazer that hungry. Not even I. My stomach is shapely as a curved leaf. (There is a goddess who slinks about the graveyard, wearing a garland of human skulls and a girdle of arms, but her stomach remains hungry flat, even with the plumpest blood.) Will you still enter my story, *Readerji?*

Yes that's *Him*, my husband. *He* walks ahead of me. I sway, slightly behind, like Queen Sita, who walked a few paces behind her Lord Rama. And I am as resolute in my vocation as she was. Sita and I are true wives.

Whether it was at their Ayodhya Palace or when Lord Rama was banished to the forest for fourteen years, Sita knew her position, and followed her husband, quick march. Even though Lord Rama pleaded, "Situ, my darling" (*He* too calls me Situ, *Readerji*), "This banishment is no camping trip. Demons roam the untrampled forest and your creamy feet thus far have felt the scratch of satin." Sita disobeyed by sweet lobbying at the palace and won. Without the dew which only comes from honouring her husband, she would become husk dry, she lamented; her seat was at her Rama's lotus feet which translates to a few steps behind. The gap from her to her Lord filled with driving love.

But I am a modern day Sita. I follow *Him* languidly with a touch of hips, when *He* opens the door for me. *He* stops, *His* hand powder light on my back. I glide toward our seats. *He* uses his fingertips to remove my coat. It comes off, straight as a margin. I shift my legs slightly to the left. My ankles are scooped of any thickness. Above my heels, the saffron-gold strap hollows where my flesh concaves; the bone between shining nimbly. Every other day, I soak my feet in lemon water.

I look around lazily, tartly, secure as a child at her pole-game. The child who teases and coaxes her enemy but at the slightest sign of danger, scurries to her pole and touches it . . . safe. *He* is reading *His* program. I want to talk but I don't. Honour and duty are tight packages that haven't gone bad in me. Frozen fresh and then thawed just . . . just, ah! perfect.

There is a bulky man across the aisle staring up. His jacket is so tight. I am afraid the man's jacket will tear if he keeps craning his neck so high; he can't get enough of the ceiling. What's up there? Nothing. The ceiling is high and its middle is a vast hole. The man in the tight jacket is getting restless. He reminds me of a bird, twitching his head right, then left, then right again. I can't see much of the woman beside him, because he is blocking her, only coffee-silk patches of her dress. I know she is his wife. Look at the way she sits, *Readerji*, close to him and yet she has nothing to do with him. The silk across her shoulders is clenched as teeth. The man in the tight jacket is getting to his wife.

Excuse me *Readerji*, but *He* has finished reading the program. And your interest, I see, has reverted to the woman in the ivory dress. Her banquet back full of wine and an unfinished gazer. But she must not turn around. Ah, so now I have triggered your interest. If she turns around, *Readerji*, you may finish her. Hunger does that. But press your forehead against her back, I swear your brow will turn holy. Don't you know that in lofty intimacy, seduction reels bell-pitch (my courtesan lesson to you, *Readerji*). Let me tell you that devotee Mira who married herself to Krishna, the blue God, and Therese of Lisieux weren't God-crazed for nothing!

Readerji, what's with the invisible frown of yours? It resembles *His*. Relax, I'm not God-sexed. *Readerji*, you hunger for bedroom women in your dream and then become afraid of a heart beat. That's why you are dangerous to the woman with the ivory back. What if she unleashes her passion and you turn away, scared stiff or incapable? Then she will collapse outside your thin heart, an ill froth.

What's not written on her back is her murder. Don't ask, by whom. Because you are incapable of her passion, even fearing her, don't give her nervous names like *fitna*: the same word for beauty as well as chaos. It is a masculine load. She can make you bleed, penetrating your soul (which I call hymen) and bathe every twitch in religion. *Readerji*, are you brave enough to receive such grace? Otherwise, leave her alone.

When I was young, Grandmother rubbed my hair with coconut oil and like an ancient Chinese master repeated, over and over again, "Toast your eye on the invisible, all visible is cataract vision." Let it be, let it be *Readerji*. What do you know of a heart beat? I have even given *His* frown (and yours, *Readerji*) a colour. Purple. Purple is a body bang. Purple is frozen meat before it is warmed under a coaxing fire.

Readerji, *He* is solemnest at a play, though I haven't quite lost my anxiety when the stage churns out another Falstaff, weaker than a Las Vegas drink. *He* has this slow-slow voice he uses when I fail to retain the pink colour of shrimp. "You have ruined its compass delicacy, Sita," he tells me slow-slow, dentist slow. No longer am I *His* Situ. I rush off to the fish place on Kensington and start all over again, with prayer in my mouth.

Really, I don't have to worry. Whether it is a Falstaff, weaker than a Vegas gin & tonic or a wrathful Sita in the Ramayana, commanding Mother Earth to tear open her womb and swallow her. A hot-hot topic among the Ayodhyans. You know, the *National Enquirer* type, "Did Situ's chastity melt in Lanka?" the island of her abductor, the demon King. Sita is furious. But first things first, before she is taken into the belly of Mother Earth, she makes the Ayodhyans eat their jabber shit and becomes a first class goddess, Sita *Devi*, when she suavely walks through the circle of fire (ancient lie detector) and comes out intact. Chastity glowing on her *devi*-woman. (I picture Sita, powerful as highway lights, striding out of the fire with a glass of hot milk for Rama: innocent, nourishing, and busy.) I tell you *Readerji*, in lofty intimacy, the *devi*-martyr-heroine rides on peaks and brinks. And infinite to boot! Whenever Rama's Situ is on stage, *His* red nostrils flare with pleasure. (The colour of pleasure is red.) But *Readerji*, what makes me shake is a throbbing balcony, you know, the Romeo-Juliet/Heer-Ranjha/Laila-Majnu kind. The giddy lovers drink out of each other's necks, unheedful of poison and laugh in Yama-Death's face, "Screw you," and back to each other's necks. Then each purple couple is unmangled. Sometimes they are found in a vault, sometimes in the desert, sometimes in the *bazaari* republic. Such love makes me break out in a cold sweat. I am not ready to die. Once, there was a love I carried inside me. A giddy burden. When my breasts began to ripen, there was bunchy noise sucking my skin. *Readerji*, you have turned white. You are leaving! . . . Returning because you must check out the end. But I must check on *Him* first.

Is *He* getting impatient? Not to worry, *His* back is royal straight. It means *He* is relaxed, at play. And I, content and bold as a bird cleaning a crocodile's teeth. Peck, peck. A fat feed. My neck basking in a *Pashmena* shawl — so many feathers gathered bit by bit for me.

Once I was well-fed. Slippery as fish oil. "Finished." That's what I said to myself then, "Finished." But what a strange word, *Readerji*. It reminds me of molars. These teeth, way back. *Readerji*, you are staring at my side teeth, like a camera's penchant for side teeth. Do my teeth terrorize you? Oh, don't shy away from me now, *Readerji*, you have witnessed all my teeth, milky as well as the sly pearls.

Like teeth, finish comes in different shapes to facilitate chewing, pulping. Like the time *He* asked me, " Is it finished, now?" That night, *He* removed my shoe tenderly and clasped my foot in *His* armpit. My scraped navel burnt. But I fell in love with *Him*, harder. Slicing does that. And when *He* comes out, he goes cottony and says, "Situ, I'm finished." It's a sweet feeling grasping *His* tiredness. I am warm with the various hearts of finish.

Although there is no word for woman-finish in Sita's dictionary. But I have experienced finish too, a long time back, when *He* was in college. And I waiting for *Him*.

Then the word came out guttural, not from my throat but my navel, place of threads. Finish then was a gray raincoat with no buttons. With hair still greasy and so much love wetting my armpits, I wrote away to him, furiously, at the back of a phone bill. There was too much love to wait, to stop, shaky pen, shaky rush, screech, risen crazy. The gray raincoat swam fatly around me as I waddled to the mailbox. Finished. Sometimes at five in the morning, *He* tugs my shoulder. I don't sway toward *Him* at once. In the middle, I break in two — I am a dancer, my front as far away from *Him* as possible, but my legs taut, close to *His*. *His* second tug is heavier, lower lip heavy. *He* licks the moles on my back, all four. I am lazy then, oyster oil lazy.

"Throw away the decomposed thing," *He* tells me. Sita lobbied for freedom (sweet but tough) within the Ayodhyan palace: wife by husband, guts, belly and all, and this certainly included visa residency in the wild forests, with Rama her Lord, tamer of disorder. Sita disobeyed her Rama once and I won't throw away my coat. If I obey then I will squelch my navel threads. What if the woman in the ivory dress turns? She would be finished. I would be finished if I threw away my coat. My face would show. Play over. I prefer to be the child at her pole game. At the slightest sign of danger, she scurries to her pole and touches it . . . safe.

Readerji, you have become an Ayodhyan gossiper, dig-digging my ear. Go sit in the verandah. Rub coconut oil in your hair. Then close your eyes to read the invisible. Just as the turned-away face of the woman in the ivory dress, some things must remain private, even from the reader. Now you are becoming persistent as the damned Ayodhyans. Yes, I love *Him* harder than any damn fetus. But *Readerji*, I play better than *Him*. Fatal. Superb.

In a few moments, I will disappear. And your gaze gets hungrier, *Readerji*. Don't tear her from her *zenana* privacy. You will finish her.

Ease up, *Readerji*. Let's concentrate on the man in the tight jacket. Why does he look dead? His eyes are open. His wife is talking into his neck. But the man in the tight jacket is impervious to her, slack, now he yawns. Wife's mouth flaps open and shut — a cartoon character in a comic strip.

He will never be like the man in the tight jacket. *He* will never die in me; *He* loves me tight. I turn to *Him*. My navel swells warm. I whisper in his ear. Lick an ice cream cone. *He* nods and stares straight on at the unlit stage. *Readerji!* God, don't! Let me cool your hand. It must.

Look! Look *Readerji*, the curtain lifts.

Shabnam's Secret

The high sun blasts hot air in the shadiest spot. Town's swollen with fat, afternoon sleep. But Shabnam is not sleepy. And neither are the men at the Lion's Billiard and Paan House. They are waiting for Shabnam. The guru-padshah of the lot at the Paan House is Lion-Sher Singh, where his recital

> When Shaboo walks
> I repeat *Yaaro*-Friends
> When Shaboo walks
> She slices air
> She
> Slices
> Air

is taken over by wild applause, and one of them says to Sher Singh, "*Wah!* Guru *wah!* If the sweaty ceiling of this audience-hall slumps from new Shaboo moisture, don't lay it on us!"

"*Ooi*, even I'm scared of the mighty Rabaa," Sher Singh says, raising both hands to the sky. "How can I slander blame on you? Don't I know my Shaboo is chaos?"

"On seeing her, my limbs take on locomotion-commotion. *Guruji*, I am finished!" says Bairam, the Pandit's son.

"Bairam-child, you don't have to sit under Buddha's tree to know of woman chaos. *Yaroo*, Shaboo gets down to business, lower, to my liver. . . ."

"*Guruji*, and lo-lo-lower still." A whooping laughter in the Paan House.

Shabnam doesn't have milky wrists like Nishad's or the other town girls. At the temple, old women hold Nishad's chin between their fingers and say that it will be a lucky mother-in-law who slips bridal bangles on her creamy wrists. Nishad lets her wrists droop in their hands but her eyes take on a fleshy shyness, indissoluble. If Nishad was named Shabnam, she would have been honest to the name: *shabnam*: the moist beadwork on plump, morning flowers . . . their deft exit even when the waking sun is thin, thin as a hair strand. Lion-Sher Singh is truthful. When Shabnam walks in the bazaar, her hips slice the air and men shudder.

On this peppery afternoon, after a showdown with Feroz, her current boyfriend from Bombay, Shabnam makes a stop at Nishad's. Heads straight to the kitchen entrance. *Auntiji* is always in the kitchen.

"Hello-o-o *Auntiji*, Nishad home?"

All college girls call their friends' mothers aunty. When Nishad's mother hears this the first time, she wipes her wet nose, which trickles either way, when she giggles or is upset.

"Shabnam-daughter, this *Englis istyle* of calling me aunty makes me feel ripe naked like memsahibs at the *iswimin* pool."

So now Shabnam adds the respectful *ji* and calls her *Auntiji*. She likes the flavour it gives. Of Queen Elizabeth's English lined with green mint chutney.

"*Ooi* Shabnam-daughter, where did you spring from? Here, fresh-hot *chapatti*. You eat one, yes? I have sent her on an errand."

"*Nahi Auntiji*, my stomach feels like lead with the canteen coffee."

"Coffee, pah! Only South Indians drink coffee all day long. What you think you have the moon complexion of a goddess that you can stain it? With your dark skin, we already have difficulty in getting you an A-class groom. If your mother was alive, she would buy extra milk and rub boiled cream on your body, day and night."

"*Auntiji*, your day isn't done until you give me a six-yard lecture."

"And who says that Dark Krishna isn't Mother Yoshoda's though he never slid out of her? I have all right on you, my dark rabbit."

"I know. But don't say mother is dead."

"She is to me. Letting you deal with the thick juice from the tongues of the town-*wallahs* when she ran off with the city tailor. An un-woman. So good as dead." *Auntiji* wipes her nose with her pallauv. "Choosing herself first, over widowhood, over child. Bah! Let's push this old talk behind. Fetch me the sugar pot."

"Why blame her? To be tied to a hot kitchen. No flowers in hair, no man, forever. . . ."

"What you talking child? I am a widow, one day left, just like that, with the choking burden of my unwed Nishad. When a man dies, his woman's moisture must dry. That's the way."

"*Ooi Auntiji*, see! Tap water goes on strike but not your eyes! Come, wipe them. But mother was so young when it happened. You know, when my knobby breasts stuck out first-first, she just stared at them."

"And her heel weakened and off with the tailor. Sticking you in the temple guest house. And I don't want to hear that she pays for your lodging. Doesn't she know you need a husband to earn your own woman-house?"

"*Auntiji*, so get me a dark groom, and I will stop drinking your blood also."

"Oh, you make my nose run. This sharp tongue of yours!"

"The town-*wallahs* thrive on it. I bet if I brought out a magazine full of Shabnam answer-swings, it would sell hotter than a *filmi* gossip magazine. *Auntiji*, It is your good luck I don't provide you with a sample of my fast-fast tongue. Where did you send this Nishad?"

"To the bazaar to buy brinjals. Now this is new. Her offering to go."

"*Auntiji*, this marriage-baggage pressure of yours makes her stay out of your way."

"I tell you, these five-six weeks, all day long that girl just sleeps with hands pressed to her stomach. I ask her, 'Are you ill? If you don't want to see *Daaktar* Rahim, let me at least see where it hurts.' Here, my hair goes grey with worry and the memsahib just turns her back and faces the wall. If Nishad's father was alive, she wouldn't have dared."

"Sometimes, the way you go after her is too much."

"During these slippery years of my daughter's life, my husband has to die on me."

"And it isn't Nishad's fault, *Auntiji*."

"I should have been firm and married her off long ago. But what to do? These days, boys want college-returned brides. What a waste! These college-*vollege* days, you while away your time at the dirty canteen and then speak *Englis* at home, faster than the *Englis* can twitter themselves, I tell you Shabnam, this high pitched jabber eats my brain away. And now this new fangled habit of sleeping all day. Sugared *chapatti?*"

"*Auntiji*, relax doubly now that you have told me. I'll get it out of her. Even with me she has been *gum-sum* quiet. But *Auntiji*, slack off hammering on marriage for a few idle days. *Hai*, your *chapatti* is soft as a hankie."

When *Auntiji* sees Shabnam eating her rolled *chapatti* dripping with butter and brown sugar, she asks, "Where is your heaving stomach now?"

Shabnam bites into the roll, sharp white bites. "Gone to the temple dogs."

"Shabnam-daughter, be at peace. At least whilst eating."

Shabnam tells Feroz that she will go to his flat only if she can bring her girlfriend. But Feroz has conditions: "Not a tight-laced one but a fun-fun baby."

"Someone like me? An open-open one. You know, the *chalu*-fast sort?"

"Shabnam, I swear upon pure Allah. . . ."

"What is purest is your itch, my villain from Bombay."

"*Hai*, you know how to finish a man! Bone aside, you suck my marrow. Shabnam, others you finish with your famous hips but I am finished by your sword-tongue."

"*Yaar*, have you men usurped Omar Khayyam's gully? Your mouths red from the Paan House wine, spewing Taiwan-repros of the *Ustad's* verses. I want to watch the video at your flat and I am bringing Nishad."

"With her around, I won't be able to come near you. Shabnam, you want to kill me waiting for you?"

"My villain from Bombay, your itch won't let you."

"Nishad*ji* won't come."

"Feroz, this *ji* polite decoration is getting to me. You think purity A-A brand only gushes out of Nishad *ji?* Is it because she behaves bride-tight? Then you haven't gotten over sucking from a bottle! First lesson, my villain *ji*, Nishad and I are the same inside. Didn't your own Prophet say that when you feel the itch, best do it with your wife, as all women are same inside. We have the same hunger until your man-tribe teaches us who climbs and who makes chapatti."

"How dare you take the Prophet's name in vain? If there were others like you available, you wouldn't get a chance to set foot on my door step!"

"True-true my villain from Bombay, but right now, I call the shots. You shouldn't have told me so much about hot-hot Rohima Wakil, I have to watch that video. Your choice."

"What choice?"

"Now, if I leaked all in one day, my price would lose tightness."

I am dying to see the banned video, *Inside Veiled Quarters*, that Feroz smuggled from Dubai. But I can't see it alone with Feroz. He would swallow me. Nishad *must* come. God, I want to see Rohima Wakil do it all! *Flesher* exposed Rohima in gully-gully of India! That her nipples are the colour of betel nut, and the cluster of blue spots on her right thigh.

And the hot-*masala* commotion between the director and Rohima. Rohima absolutely no-no-no — she wouldn't do the sex scenes strictly in her birthday suit. She needed heavy gold jewellery. When the director brings in stuff about honouring the role of a young maharanee widow, whose prime widow duty would be to shear all gold from her royal body, Rohima gives him two options: to fetch a live maharanee and let her do a *pucca*-authentic portrayal or to let her, Rohima, get on with her work in thick clasping jewellery. The director resigns to the latter. *Wah!* Rohima, My Guru! Us *chalu*-free ones call the shots. Feroz says the scenes burnt him finished. "That Rohima is a *Kama Sutra* gymnast."

It is pointless waiting for Nishad here. What if Nishad says a flat no? Maybe she won't. Last month, in the canteen, when I sneaked in a copy of *Flesher* for her, her eyes stuck like glue on the print. And her open mouth. The only thing is to get Feroz out of his flat. Then Nishad will agree. Let Nishad request Feroz to leave the flat for a few hours . . . after all he calls her Nishad*ji*. No, he won't know how to refuse her. But will Nishad agree to this? I should go to the bazaar where we can argue privately, in English.

"*Aree* Shabnam, where are you going? What will I do with this?" A new sugared chapatti droops out of *Auntiji's* hand.

"Later *Auntiji*, I am going to track her down in the bazaar."

"Of course leave in all haste."

"*Auntiji*, now I am gone, and now we will both be back, *fatafat*."

"And *fatafat* with my brinjals. It seems like the girl has gone to grow brinjals! Come quick, I don't want to die in this boiler room waiting for the damn vegetable. You hear?"

The grimy window of the Lion's Billiard and Paan House is choked with hot, musky vapours. The oglers watch those famous hips drawing close. In the Paan House, a young boy, barely thirteen, soaks in the jumbled smells of hair, cigarette, and sour sweat. Wanting to be part of the show, he asks the Guru, "Is Shabnam more beautiful than the dancing women who entertain Gods?"

A giddy laughter fills the place, and the muscled Sher Singh rises. "Come here laddie, your lesson is about to begin."

As she approaches the Paan House, Shabnam's hips move jauntily and her whole body collects an arched tautness. But her eyes are lazy. The boy is shoved out of the Paan House and left on the steps, his shirt pulled to one shoulder in the shove. He hesitates for a long while and then rushes toward Shabnam and splutters out an excited speech drilled into him by Sher Singh. "Shaboo, my Shaboo, I have woken. . . ."

Shabnam stares at him without a flinch. Stares at his Adam's apple bob and bob. His face crumples and he rushes back into the Paan House. But at the door, Sher Singh catches his thin shoulders and leads him back to Shabnam. The gang of oglers follow.

"Hey laddie, if you operate like this, there is no hope for you. You aren't a Man without being approved by our Shaboo. *Ooi* Shaboo, how goes it? Those hips can kill."

"This morning, I heard my hips finish men."

"I place a new devotee at your feet. His face still soft with hair."

"Be it a circumcised one, or a turbaned one, or Bairam full of priestly ghee, what difference is it to me? What difference is it to me that you want to corrupt a twelve-year old?"

"*Ooi* Shaboo, what dirty words from my she-Guru's mouth, who's talking corruption? This laddie awaits initiation. But let him wait. I am parched waiting for you."

"It's a pity your intelligence isn't as large as your frame, Sher Singh. Who else will look for dew in this beating sun?"

There is a lot of thigh slapping from the crowd.

"Careful Shabnam, your tongue is getting sharp."

"Slit sharp. Tell you what, when your mother picks out a bride for you, a model Sita*ji*-pure. Exercise on her your divine right. Scissor her speech thin to your heart's content. But send her to me for the walk."

Unhastily Shabnam breaks away from the party, walks onwards to the market. The afternoon wind hitches her top shirt higher, and a slice of her curved inner thigh is sharp under her thin, cotton pyjamas. Her swinging hips cut the way.

It is Bairam who breaks the humiliated silence. "This time Shabnam has gone too far. How dare she bring Mother Sher Singh's name on her foul tongue."

Sher Singh spits loudly. Wipes his mouth. "The whore will have to pass my garage sooner or later."

In the bobbing market place, Shabnam can't find Nishad. Just screams of cajolers and discontented buyers. Shabnam stands by the brinjal stall. A slight woman in a starched cotton sari hesitates over the brinjals. The dirty turbaned seller pleads with her. "Okay sister, six brinjals for two rupees. I can't make it less. It would mean snatching food from my childrens' mouths."

Even while bargaining, the clean woman's eyes remain downcast. Then as if pulled by force, the brinjal seller's head jerks sideways, and Shabnam's eyes pour hard into his. His eyes widen and gleam moistly. Shabnam leaves the bazaar.

She knows better than to pass Sher Singh's garage today. She follows another way to get to the temple guest-house. Past the rice fields, past the town's sewage system, and over the bridge, she enters the narrow and hushed street. Although there are shops here, nothing is displayed in the windows. And then Shabnam sees Nishad coming down the steep steps of the cobwebbed brown building where there is only Datta Dani's office. There is only one reason why anyone visits Datta Dani.

He calls it an office. And his helpers aren't from town. Datta Dani wears thin red gloves. Shabnam can't move. She knows that like death, the brown building which Nishad is emerging from is a one-way direction. When one is heavy and four-legged, and doesn't want to remain this way, one visits Datta Dani here, and comes out two-legged.

"My *Auntiji*, you will never know of this. I promise!"

You will never know, forever, my promise. Now on, the sting of your salt tears will dry inside my raw pear stomach, daughter stomach. Nishad, no don't turn around. Your basket of purple brinjals and gouged out wound, yours, only for this day. For I am behind you like Lord Krishna, holding out an eternal sari. Yes, like Krishna covers Draupadi in the Court-Hall of the Kauravas. I won't let Feroz or Sher Singh near you. Remember Nishad? By baring Draupadi, the Kauravas would ram the honour of the Draupadi-Pandava clan back into their teeth. But Draupadi prays to her Krishna. As Draupadi spins, yards and yards of stripped sari fall to the floor of the Kaurava Court, balanced by sari, colour after colour, swimming out of the dark God's palm, onto Draupadi's waist. Your bridal wrists will remain announced as ever, for I am your she-Krishna.

But Nishad, who caught who? Last week we saw the red gloves in his empty car, sticking out under the driver's seat, new and polythene covered. You looked at them tenderly, without haste. Unnerved by your strange face, I spewed, "Someone's pinkie must have worked hard." You turned and held my face. Your salt mother face, not shunning, like mother's shun, when she found my loins in the tailor's eye, in *his* eye. Sweet Nishad*ji*, you caught me: "Shabnam, you have never done it, have you? Your dirty mouth full of purity."

Lion's Granddaughter

I have two shillings. With my index finger, I hook one shilling and with my middle finger, I hook the other shilling. The thick, perfect coins lie snug in my frock pocket. I am going to Piccadilly Household and Sundries to buy Katherine's present. Miss Rice, our newest teacher at Stockley, when she first comes to know of Piccadilly Household and Sundries said, "Good Gracious! Piccadilly in midst of Central Tanzania." I like Miss Rice. She wears a lot of blue dresses with pink piping, and if she presses her hand too hard on the table, it turns red. I never turn red. I am the darkest girl in my new school.

The old school is in the middle of town, opposite Mr. Birbal's carpentry shop. Sometimes, even after school, the zing-zing from his shop hums in my ears.

At the old school, I am invited to birthday parties, even Nagib Rehman's, who doesn't like me. I am invited because I am the Lion's Granddaughter.

Grandmother presses my pink party dress, then she hangs it in the cupboard again, because I don't go. I never bother with the presents, especially Nagib's. Grandfather buys the presents from Household and Sundries. They are always gold wrapped and carry Grandfather's seal: a green lion. Green is the Prophet's colour. The postman collects the parcels from Grandfather in the study until Grandmother put a stop to it.

"Your arrogance will be the death of this child! I have grieved enough for her mother. Listen well, Grandfather of Chiku, she will not go to parties nor will you send presents on her behalf."

Only Grandmother and Chief Juma call me Chiku, like the sweet fruit. Grandfather and Mummy call me by my real name, Aisha.

Whenever Grandmother is upset, she brings Mummy in. Grandfather does not say anything but returns to work. Then it is Grandmother who brings tea to his study and not Chief Juma. And in the evening, she allows me to go with Grandfather to the Dodoma Club. I wear my pink dress then.

My hair is not straight like other girls. They tie three knots in their ribbons before the final bow. I don't have to tie even one knot because nothing slides out of my hair. I throw away the blue ribbons when I come to Stockley. We do not wear uniforms at Stockley.

Grandmother tries to keep my knotty hair smooth. Every night, before I go to bed, she rubs my scalp and stretches all the roots with coconut oil boiled in rose petals. I am the only half-half in Dodoma.

Whenever I pass Nagib Rehman, he sings:

Miss half-half
so hoity-toity
Black skin tight
left, right
left, right
About turn!

Nagib's clothes smell of fried fish. Mrs. Rehman cooks for bachelors and boarders. And if there is a death in town, Grandfather goes to pick up Mrs. Rehman, who sits at the back, as if she is in a proper taxi. She cooks the large town meal of rice and *dal* in the kitchens of the Mosque. Grandfather donates sacks and sacks of rice to the Mosque. The funeral meal is eaten after the men return from the cemetery.

Nagib does not like anyone mentioning about his father, though everyone knows. Mr. Rehman remains straight sober only on Fridays, Mosque-Day. Sometimes, Mrs. Rehman waits outside Grandfather's study and after offering her a cup of tea, he sends Chief Juma to fetch Mr. Rehman from the Tusker Bar.

Grandfather says only Chief Juma can coax a crocodile to unscrew its jaws and let his supper hop out. And only Chief Juma can persuade Mr. Rehman to leave the bar. Grandfather says that Juma will drink an ocean of secrets and never let out even a burp. That's why Grandfather calls him Chief Juma.

One day, Grandfather gives me eighty shillings for the Fee Master, "And tell the Fee Master that forty shillings is for Nagib Rehman."

I pay my fee in the morning then wait until recess when the class gathers under the mango tree for a game of marbles. When it's Nagib's turn, I block the game, "My Grandfather says to give you fee money." Nagib stares at me, hard. His eyes gleam shiny. I think he will cry. He does not. He takes the money and puts it in his pocket and then spits on the ground. It does not matter to me. I buy a Coke and freshly roasted peanuts.

At Stockley everyone is different. Kristjana is from Iceland. None of us know much about Iceland, so Miss Rice asks Kristjana to read us an Icelandic story. Now I know what fjords are. But they make me think of milkshakes. It is the "j" in fjord. F-i-o-r-d is a spiky river between tall cliffs, but fjord is foam, a slab of foam topping a milkshake. And Kristjana's story makes me hungry for tomatoes.

On this island, there are no vegetables, only fish. I remember what the girl in the story says. "And in summers we graze like sheep among the mountain grasses." Even daisies. She plucks and eats the daisies.

But I cannot forget how the girl in the back seat of her mother's car eats all the tomatoes. One by one, out of a brown bag. She eats them soundlessly.

Now, before afternoon tea, I eat tomatoes from Iceland.

Chief Juma says, "*Weh* Chiku, drop your fridgeland, these tomatoes are from the market."

"Chief Juma, this fruit is only for the Goddesses of Iceland."

"What is the Lion up to? Sending you to that fancy school to learn about tomatoes."

Chief Juma's knife has a rusty handle. He picks a tomato with overspilling cheeks and cuts it almost in two. He pushes in salt and pepper, rubs them together, then tears them apart. The juice runs down my elbow. I want to eat soundlessly like the girl in the back seat but there is too much juice, and I have to slurp to hold it back.

When I break my right arm, falling from a tree, Miss Rice gives me red stars for writing a verse with my left hand. "And polish off this one, too," she says, giving me another verse to copy. Now I do sums with my right hand but if I want to write something on a card, I use my left hand and watch the letters come off slightly slanted, large as teeth. Inside the green margin of my notebook, Miss Rice writes, "Brook clear work. Keep it up!"

It is after recorder lesson when Katherine invites me to her birthday party. She pulls out a penknife from her pocket and slips the string over her shoulder. "It's an early present from Daddy. He had to leave right away because of the elephant herds. They are leaving the Serengeti Park and moving toward the coffee plantations." Katherine's father is the Park's Commissioner.

"Will you come to my party on Friday?" Katherine asks.

My heart beats so hard that I hold my shoulder.

"I can't. I think my brother will be coming home then."

"You have a brother?"

"Of course. In Dar es Salaam, at the boarding school."

"I didn't know you had a brother. What if he isn't here by Friday, will you come then?"

"You can never tell with him."

"Mummy will be taking us to Simba Hill, and. . . ."

"Simba Hill? But one has to spend the night up there."

"And I shan't sleep until I see a lion — Oh, I wish you would change your mind. You and I can sleep in Daddy's famous orange tent which was genuinely sniffed at, by a lion."

"Was Mr. Smith inside the tent?"

"Of course not, silly. He was watching from a distance. Daddy's group was studying the behaviour of lions during the drought. And he has left the special tent for me for the Simba trip!"

After Independence, President Nyerere gives Grandfather the title of Lion, *Simba* in Kiswahili, after Simba Hill.

My heart makes noises. I do want to go to Katherine's party on Grandfather's hill.

"Katherine, I don't have a brother. I frogged out the story."

"You are awfully good at stories."

I don't say anything.

"Your caves have doors in them and creepy stuff like the boy whose stomach begins at the neck. And honestly, I hate fibs."

Now I carefully place the recorder in its case. I won't be invited. My heart isn't pounding anymore.

"But you are a whiz story maker. Can you concoct a name for your brother?"

"Ibn Shah Mohammed Ali Zafar Bogus Weakfish."

"And what does he do in Dar es Salaam?"

"He drinks a lot of coconut water, I guess."

Katherine says, "You are queer, honestly."

A bright invitation follows by post. It has a picture of a howling lion inside an orange moon. In Kwasi Idi's autograph book, under the column of "Who is Your Best Friend?" I put down, "Katherine Claire Smith of Kilimanjaro Mansion, Ascot Road, Dodoma, Tanzania, East Africa."

I am going to Piccadilly Household and Sundries to buy Katherine's present, and with my very own money. Grandmother thinks I should give her something in gold. "Not only does it show merit-weight but it's also auspicious. See this brooch? It is a princess' shoe. Now give this to your Katrin."

"I can't Grandmother, I want it to be special . . . orange, and she doesn't like brooches and stuff. Even her ears aren't pierced!"

"Hah, how can a girl's beauty show if her ears aren't pierced?"

I polish grandfather's brown shoes and spray all the twelve bedrooms with DDT. But the nastiest job is helping Grandmother sew the fold on a new sari.

"And now you understand when I tell you that money doesn't grow on trees," Grandmother says.

The fold keeps sliding out my fingers. "It's too slippery," I tell her.

"Hah! And when your mother-in-law asks me, 'How come Chiku doesn't know how to cook or sew?' I will direct her to your Grandfather's study."

Grandfather offers me extra shillings. Grandfather always uses the royal "We" when he wants to please Grandmother or me.

"Our black one, here is *baksheesh* for the polished new shoes.

Not only do We see our beard but also our eyes in them. Let us show them to Chief Juma."

"Please Grandfather, don't be indulgent. Two shillings will suffice. It's my very own true present for Katherine."

"Well then, will Our Granddaughter have dinner with us at the Club? We promise her a glass of wine."

"Of course, spoil the child — wine indeed. I am powerless to stitch up the town's mouth. Let the *town-wallahs* point their finger at us and rightly so! Wine in a Muslim's house. Yes, the Dark Age has truly come."

"Let the town go pound sand. But we ask you *Wifeji*, is feeding our grandchild spoiling her? *Wifeji*, you too, come to the Club."

"And who will go to Mosque? Useless to remind you that you haven't set foot in the Mosque for ages."

"Are you cross with Us *Wifeji?* Already We are uncomfortable."

"Then put four teaspoons of sugar in your tea. You and discomfort, *hah!* That will be my blessed day."

"Take two sweet dishes: one from Us. Next Friday, *Inshallah*, We will join Our *Wife-Begum* at the Mosque."

Grandmother only looks at him crossly. But she always takes two sweet dishes to the Mosque. Grandfather's is the best. She fills his dish with cashew nuts, almonds, pomegranates, grapes, and imported Swiss chocolates.

I call dinner with Grandfather at the Dodoma Club a private engagement. No Chief Juma or Grandmother to tell me what to do. The only time it isn't a treat at the Club is when Mummy is here. She looks at me puzzled and then brushes my hair. I wait until both Grandfather and Mummy are seated, and then sit beside Grandfather. Only Grandmother can touch my hair.

When I squint, there are stars in my wine. Grandfather doesn't know I get a sore throat from the wine. The side plates and the dinner plates have a gold rim.

"Grandfather, you are known to everyone as Simba, the Lion."

"Simba Hill is Simba Hill, and yet has anyone seen a lion up there?"

Whenever Grandfather issues a twisted language, you must think hard.

"Grandfather, why didn't you send me to Stockley Avenue earlier on?"

"Everything is ours now: first class rail bookings; the Dodoma Club and your Stockley, too." On its lawn, the Club has a bottle of Vat '69 reaching its roof.

"Why can't Nagib Rehman go to Stockley?" I know Nagib Rehman can't ever come to my new school but I like to ask anyway.

Grandfather puts down his fork and knife. "*Uhuru* certainly means independence from the British, but *Uhuru* plus *hela* makes one a very free citizen," he says, rubbing in thumb and finger. Then he piles the rice pilaff on the tip of his fork.

"Grandfather, I am very happy we have *hela-hela*."

"My black one, you are special."

"Nothing can happen to me because *you* are my Grandfather. Can we have a swimming pool? Katherine has a swimming pool."

"Hah, I am no European to bask in frivolous water in his backyard. I keep a well for crops and food."

Some people enter the lounge. It is them, the Jaffer boys. I pile my legs, one on top of another, like a filmstar. I know they stare at me when grandfather isn't looking. I sip my wine, careful about the long stem.

The shillings jingle in my pocket. There is hardly anyone about this morning. Even the market square is empty. I like it when the square is full of shrieks, especially when Ramson's black cinema van with glossy posters glides around announcing the release of the new Sunday film. The heroine sings to the blue sky. Sometimes a deer follows her. But she doesn't know that the hero is watching her. The hero is always from the city, carrying a camera and wearing safari boots. Later he will take the heroine to the city, and that's the exciting part, when she is transformed into a real heroine. He teaches her the Twist. Her hair is cut shoulder length and she has a fringe. When the heroine gets under the table to prick a lost pea with her fork, the audience roars. The hero teaches the heroine three things: how to eat with a fork and a knife, the Twist, and how to wear mini skirts and hipster saris. Under each poster, the familiar and wonderful words follow: "action," "drama," "suspense," "fights," and always, always there is "tender romance."

The Zebra Crossing is approaching fast so I walk slower than a snail. A car roars and slyly I turn my head. But it isn't them, the Jaffer boys. They are famous for stopping their Red, Rackety, Roofless 3-R Car, barely four inches from the Crossing. Normally, the girls screech, but when they did it to Katherine and me, we stared back, and through their split windshield, they saluted.

I can't linger at the Crossing any longer and cross the street.

"Look where the sun has risen from today?" Mr. Jeevan says when I enter his shop. In town, he is known as Jeevan-Peanuts. For the longest time he sold roasted peanuts outside the Mosque and school grounds. Mr. Jeevan bought Piccadilly Household after *Uhuru*. He has two tailors outside. Miss Rice has her dresses stitched here. Threads hang from Mr. Jeevan's hair and much of his lower lip is thrust outward where tiny spit sways.

"At my humble step, almost the *Lionji* himself, no?"

"My name is Aisha."

"Aisha, *wah!* Such a grand name. You know what it means?"

"Hope."

"Who named you?"

"Mummy."

"I thought Bharmal the Lion named you — he is always insisting on change, on hope. He told me that the name of my shop is too *Englis*."

"Mr. Jeevan, I have come to buy a. . . ."

"Ah yes, where is your mother, these days?"

"At the University of Kenya."

"You must pass her my *salaams*. Is she now teaching real stuff, like sciences and *chapa* math?"

"My mother is a painter. The Town-Hall has one of her paintings of tribal brewing of *pombe* on Simba Hill."

"*Ooi* Child, don't give me the long Koran of Dodoma history. What, all this Independence warmth swirling only in Bharmal navels?"

I want to leave, but I won't.

"Mr. Jeevan, I am looking for a hair-band, please."

"What colour, what brand? Choose UK brand, tip-top quality."

"May I see the orange one, please — no . . . no, the darker one. How much is it for?"

"*Wah!* is the Lion's grandchild discussing price with me. No, no, just take it. After all, your Grandfather sends presents to our children on their birthdays."

"You are very kind, but I am not allowed to buy anything without paying for it."

"Now, now, you tell me, Aisha-Hope, why should all charity cluster in the Lion's household? Give us small folk a chance. Forgive me," he says, holding the tips of his ears like a monkey, "I am not talking of heavy *hela* like Lion Bharmal's donation to the Dodoma Power Company or giving away lorries to self-reliant farming co-ops. Only he can afford to warm Nyerere's eye.

"The rest of us East Indians are only ants, greedily looking for sugar money."

Outside the sewing machines stop.

I whisper, "Please take my money. The hair-band is for Katherine."

"Katrin? Let us even listen who this Katrin-vatrin is."

"She is a friend of mine from Stockley Avenue School. The hair-band is a birthday present for her."

"And your Grandfather tells me the name of my shop is colonial, when you won't drink a glass of water from our houses but with naked feet run to a foreigner's dwelling. You must tell me what is wrong with our own school."

"Nothing."

"The Bharmals can't be regular folk. Do you eat pork now? I mean your Grandfather never goes to Mosque. Always at the Dodoma Club."

"I never eat pork!"

"See, what happened to your mother, Aisha-Hope?" Mr. Jeevan says, coming over to my side, "All these visits to African houses, wearing African clothes, as if only the Lion Bharmal family cel-celebrates *Uhuru*-independence. Your grandfather had it coming when a Bantu leaked swollen seeds in his hot daughter and then ran off *chapa-chapa*, full of hyena glee. And still your Lion Grandfather doesn't have the shame to tuck his tail between his legs."

There are red marks like tong burns on Mr. Jeevan's cheek. His sticky spit dries on my throbbing palm.

But when he grabs my shoulders, I shake him off easy.

"It is my mother who wears a shamed tail. But We, Sir, are the Lion's Granddaughter."

I scratch the side of my jaw where tears burn. The buildings glitter like teeth. Katherine will get a brooch on her birthday.

Peace Flats

We live in Peace Flats. After the town dump, we don't think of it as Peace Flats any more. No matter how high the sun is in the stinging sky making everything white steel so that tears come out of my prickled eyes, beyond the dump, the sun's gone purple as if it's had a good bashing. Juma lives out there. Out there, many of them have two wives. Sometimes three.

"If Juma ever looks at you here," Grandmother tells me, jabbing my chest with her strong index finger, "You come to me this instant. I'll salt his black skin and throw it to the hyenas."

Juma carries on washing clothes pretending he hasn't heard.

Grandmother has changed since the Government nationalized banks, schools, buildings, and mills, Chinese communist style. In the kitchen, as she dishes out food for Mother Hadhari, she tells her, "Indians worked hard, damn hard in the jungle-interior for years and now when we can see face of cities, buy buildings . . . we never stopped Africans from coming to school, we stashed away steadily as a heart beat, eating only *dal* and *chapatti!* Nyerere has stripped Indians *uchi*-naked and wipes his tingling penis with Mao cotton balls!"

But the Indian *jawans* protest publicly. "Everything is property of the rotund Government" is written on urinating walls by the *jawans*. Sometimes complete stories are sprayed on walls. Like the story of the sly-mother who has only one *chapatti* and two daughters. So the mother divides the *chapatti* in two, and distributes them to her daughters. The daughters won't have it and each one protests, "No *Maa*, no, here take mine." This is the story of how the mother balloons.

Before nationalization, the *jawans* hog front seats at Ramson's Cinema. In the packed house, they recite goofball couplets to the teary courtesan-heroine who confesses she is in love. They orally translate the Hindi film title in English, which sounds silly enough but in Kiswahili the translation makes your belly grow full with water laughter. On the movie poster of *Jab Jab Phool Khile*, stuck on the display window of Piccadilly Household and Sundries, the *jawans* scribble the titles in English and Kiswahili.

When When Flowers Laugh
Wakati Wakati Maua Wana Cheka

This is the only time Juma laughs with me, "Eh Shil, *vipi* Dal?" Juma hates lentils and can't understand how Indians stomach *dal* every afternoon.

I answer back, "*Vipi ugali?*" which he eats everyday. Although I like *ugali*, especially rolling the stiff porridge into a bite-sized ball and then pressing my thumb into its centre to scoop in the curry.

"*Vipi*, such a *kichwa maji* title?" Juma asks. Properly, *kichwa maji* refers to a person whose head is full of water, in other words, who has nothing up there. But it is true Hindi films in Kiswahili loose their screw and make the belly stretch with water laughter.

When Mohammed Ali loses the world title, the *jawans* shave off their heads. To protect their heads, they wear red straw hats to match their red rickety cars. But no longer is red a bride's colour. Red is China colour, so now the *jawans* paint their red cars khaki, soldier colour, and hurl plates in the Dodoma Hotel, chanting, "Everything belongs to the Government — no need to use goods gingerly!" This time the *jawans* don't let their hair grow back to protest against the Government's treatment of Indians. But Peace Flats isn't happy. The *jawans* make Peace Flats nervous. "They are dangling all Indians like carrots in front of the Government, and we have virgin daughters in our houses," Mother Hadhari says.

Grandmother said to her, "So you want them to eat *dal* and hide under the bed, like the rest of us stalwart Indians?" But Grandmother does not protest when the Government takes the *jawans* to prison on the charge of making fake passports.

I remember when Nyerere first comes to Dodoma, just after independence. Grandmother put me in front of her body and said,

"Shil, see that man," pointing to Nyerere, "He is like your uncle." I am four and begin crying because Grandmother is crying.

Before, on the radio, whenever, "*Pole, Pole Mzee. O Mama, Kenyata aleya taka Kenya*" plays, Grandmother cries. This is when Kenyata is imprisoned by the British, and Mama Makeba sings, "Sorry, Sorry Elder. O Mother, Kenyata who wanted Kenya." *(As soon as school is over, Khoti ties on his head kerchief. He wears it as a head-band which reads, "O Mother, Kenyata aleya taka Kenya." When Miss Chinua introduced Khoti to the class we giggled because of his purple socks. In Dodoma, no boy wears girl colours.)*

Now President Mao's picture hangs beside Nyerere's and things have changed. Juma spends two hours drinking morning tea. When Grandmother asks him not to have the radio on during work, he tells her, "Mama, you are asking me not to be become an informed citizen."

Mother Hadhari tells Grandmother, "A soldier yanked Indu's short dress." *(Indu is the most beautiful girl in Peace Flats.)* "Shil's Grandmother, the soldier tells our Indu, 'Come to me if you want to roam *uchi*-naked.' And your Juma was there but he just stood there and laughed with the rest of them, heh-heh-heh, his white teeth full of meat!"

"Indu hasn't been out of Peace Flats and she thinks that she is Miss UK and back. Don't know whether the Kassams realize what they are bringing to their heads sending that ripe girl to the city," Grandmother says.

Indu looks like filmstar Nanda. Even the same teeth. Like Nanda, Indu has a small tooth growing above her two side teeth. She wears pink nail varnish at school, where only "A" level students can wear nail varnish. But after her "O" levels, she leaves school. Now, she is going to Dar es Salaam to become a secretary.

In Peace Flats, we call her our UK Heer. She sings "My Boy Lollipop" at school parties. If you ask Indu if she has been to London, she smiles. In Peace Flats, we have a UK Heer and The Poet. Whenever The Poet sees Indu, he takes sand and sprinkles it on his head. Just like Ranjha did in the love story of Heer-Ranjha. In fact, she got half her name, Heer, because of The Poet's devotion to her. *(I don't laugh at love stories, anymore.)*

Sometimes Grandmother starts on Juma when he hasn't done anything to provoke, especially on weekends. Only on Royal Ascot, where foreigners live, servants work until half-twelve on Saturday. Off till Monday, like school. On Royal Ascot, they are called stewards. Also up there live the Tejpars and Kartar Singh, the Europeans' lawyer. Khoti lives on Royal Ascot. Mr. Kamanga, Khoti's father, is the Hotel Director of the New Stanley Hotel. Mr. Kamanga and Khoti are from Kenya.

Grandmother is the Chairwoman of the Peace Flats Library and annual meetings are held at the New Stanley. She tells Mother Hadhari, "Black Kenyans are sophisticated. And then, Mr. Kamanga isn't like the rest of them. He lives on Royal Ascot, and has been to Oxford."

I giggle on Mother Hadhari's pronunciation when she says, "*Hai*, you mean that big Oxfus?"

On weekends, Juma has the radio on full blast in the ironing room. No longer do we get "Namaste" and "This is the Sound of India At Your Request." Now, President Nyerere makes two-hour speeches. But the first half-hour is full of jokes.

> "Bwana has a fascinating shadow that grins and grins. Brothers and sisters, I am sitting on the pavement eating groundnuts outside New Stanley Hotel, you know, watching the Bwana tribe go in and out. Brothers and Sisters, you watch how Bwana is always touch-touching his Madam? Is she a little *mtoto* who can't cross the street without an elder? One day I'm instructed by Madam to go to the Airport to get Madam's daughter, Tina. The airport road is too choked with fumes for Madam. Madam's daughter must be sick because Madam is sending telegram after telegram to Miss Tina all the way to London-proper. I even buy a pair of white gloves to hold Miss Tina's elbow so she can cross the street. You know, like Chieftain England Queen whose subjects touch her with respect-gloves. So to give Miss Tina full respect, I put on gloves. Back of mind, I say, what if this Tina is youthful and has the white woman walk, that flying swing that her breasts go bob-a-bob! Hey, to cross the street holding London-proper bob-a-bob!"

The crowd on the radio goes "Hu-yee!" Whistles and clapping.

"Brothers and Sisters, where do Europeans stay?"

"At the New Stanley Hotel," the crowd responds altogether, just like we do in the school assembly, when we greet the teachers standing on the platform, "Good Morning, Teachers."

> "Right, Brothers and Sisters, the Hotel is named after Mr. Bwana himself, Stanley the Explorer. Yes, it is good to sit outside New Stanley eating groundnuts, watching them like bwana folk watched us not so long ago. It is good to watch white women's flesh leap. But my story has a bad ending. After all my glove parade, you may say, Brothers and Sisters, that I am forced to eat cow dung instead of *ugali-fufuo* in my soup. Oh yes, I manage to hold Tina but I hadn't expected it like this! Brothers and Sisters, I leave the Airport, carrying a sleeping dog in a small house. Tina is Madam's dog! In London, the dog reads Madam's telegrams. Brothers and Sisters, first dogs, then us!"

Now there are shrieks on the radio.

"*Mama Yangu!*" Juma says, shaking his head from side to side.

Then his shoulders bend forward with laughter.

> "So Brothers and Sisters, do I look surprised when Madam in the bush goes 'Leo! Here Leo!' to the lioness with her cubs at the water pool? Madam is braver than the Masai! Even then Shadow, Bwana's servant, doesn't stop grinning. I get irritated! I want to push him in a Masai circumcision tent this instant to make him a man fast-fast! What's the matter with this Black Brother? Does Bwana have Shadow's mother's tits that Shadow wants to latch on him all the time? Shadow's making Bwana's bed, cooking his roast beef, making a seat-box toilet in the bush so that Bwana can read in comfort. Bwana-hat, Bwana-burp, Bwana's Sunday to Sunday

> quinine. That's Brother Shadow's mother's milk. Bwana says 'Simon Says' and Shadow deep-pressed to wall, grinning 'Yes Masta.' This Black Brother has a loose penis that won't go up. Brothers and Sisters, you met this Bwana's Shadow, one grinning Black servant?"

There is hoot-hoot laughter. Wild clapping and then Nyerere's laughter takes over, high and cackling, and Grandmother says, "There is that hyena laughing. *Weh* Juma, turn him low." Juma turns down the volume.

> "Hey, don't call me President Nyerere, call me Nephew or Brother because in this freedom we are related."

The women clap their hands to their lips and go *ululululululu* like there is a wedding on.

> "Tanzania, unite in nephew-nephew blood. Look at the Chinese, all working together after removing the fat class."

"That hyena means Indians, but he goes about it his hyena way," Grandmother says.

> "Now our Chinese-nephews are here to guide us. Praise Mao. Slice the enemy, slice capitalists."

Grandmother goes to the ironing room and switches off the radio, and when she returns, her eyes only look at me when she says, "Let other Indians hug Africans. This country has become a Mecca Haj, everyone brother-brother, hah! Especially the Indian, hair passive with coconut oil, and fat with property. Well, I have no fat property Nyerere can nationalize. Or a Swiss bank account that I have to suck up to some Deputy Commissioner, give him tea money under the table!"

Juma keeps on washing. The bucket piles with wrung sausage-shaped clothes.

If you want something done to someone or want to speak to

your dead sister, only then you go beyond Peace Flats. Or when a new business begins, an auspicious coconut is broken outside the office and a cock is sacrificed beyond Peace Flats as precaution. When the orange moon is out on a thick night and the distant, steady beat of a zebra drum goes *dhoom dhoom dha DHOOM* in my eardrum, my feet turn sour cold, malaria sick. Something is being woken up out there, summoned to rise.

Mother Hadhari who does not have a left eye says that Mirza Roshan has been "done on." She says that long ago (it must be before I was born because Mirza Roshan now wears tattered trousers and when he gives you change, his hand shakes) he was one of the wealthiest goldsmiths. During the marriage season, after the long rains, on *Idd* and even the European *Idd* in December (when Piccadilly Household and Sundries had crates and crates of imported cherries) Mirza Roshan's shop was packed, you couldn't budge. It was during such an *Idd*, Mother Hadhari said that Mirza Roshan saw a beautiful woman wearing a silver veil.

"I saw her too," Mother Hadhari says. "Tall. She looked from the coast. Had that glossy coastal skin, from eating fish, I guess. She left the shop. And stood outside his display window, looking inside. Then in his cattle-packed shop, Mirza Roshan let out such a screech that it shattered his display window. A pinched whimper and then a spine shriek, that's what came out of Mirza Roshan's voice box that day, close to *Idd*."

"Mirza Roshan claimed," Mother Hadhari continued, "that in place of teeth the silver veiled woman had black nails, so many that you couldn't count, spiking out of her drained white gums, and where her tongue ought to have been, lolled an unspilling pool of blood. And it is since that day Mirza Roshan lost full interest in gold and his family, and bought a tiny shop where he sells his roasted groundnuts, milk, eggs, and torches."

When I hear drums, I don't bother with the pillow Grandmother leaves for me on her chair. She jerks when my cold feet touch hers. Turns. Lifts a leg and I pile my sour feet between her legs. Grandmother mutters, "The damn drums! If they are brewing *pombe* out there, we better not expect Juma in the morning."

Juma looks at me with angry eyes. I keep out of his way. Even when I want to wear a certain dress, I don't take it to him in the ironing room but throw it in the dry clothes hamper on the verandah. In twenty minutes, there is a knock on my door. Juma holds the pressed dress to his chest. He lays it on the bed. I don't look at him but I know that his eye gleams on my temple, steady.

It is very hot one afternoon. I am seven then. Since Grandmother is asleep, I remove my petticoat and sit under the mango tree. The rough grass is cool. I spot the green cart and run to the kitchen.

"Juma, the sugar cane cart is passing."

"Be away, I'm eating."

"But I'm thirsty.

"Drink water."

"No! Get me sugar cane, now!"

"Where is your petticoat?"

Grandmother says only shameless girls loiter without a petticoat. Juma's stare makes me sick as if I have drunk milk too fast. "Don't stare. I'll tell Grandmother."

Juma grabs me and forces me to lie on his lap. I can see his woolly head coming closer. On his lips there is grease from the beef curry. I can smell the beef rust in his mouth.

"Grandmother!" I yell. At once Juma pushes me off but not before pinching my left nipple, very hard.

"Juma, you Blackey! Grandmother will peel your skin, when I tell her!"

"And I will take you beyond Peace Flats!"

In the evening Grandmother comes into the bathroom to help me wash my hair. I keep my left hand over my strange nipple. It is blue. Grandmother is huffing. "Wash well behind your ears. Scrub your armpits, Shil."

The second time, I forget to lock the door. It is after Khoti comes to our school. Sometimes in the afternoon, when Grandmother sleeps, I take off my dress. My breasts aren't like Indu's. When she breathes, you can see them go up and down. I practice Indu's flying walk but whenever I see Khoti, my head goes down on its own.

When I am about to put on my dress, I see Juma in the mirror. His eyes stare at mine. And then he flees the room, dropping his broom. Even the threat of being taken beyond Peace Flats cannot remove my shame. Juma has seen me. Sometimes, when I think of it, I make crying noises.

Our town is like new bread. All the wonderful part, the middle, the hump, the wood-shiny crust. Best. Like Royal Ascot. The ends are just there. Well, Peace Flats is one such end. All flats here are the same. Gray on the outside with two rusty gutter poles clutching each flat in a lewd hug. The Town Council has built these flats for people like us. (But we aren't poor like Mother Hadhari. Sharp at lunch she knocks on any door in Peace Flats, where a kitchen plate is set aside for her.)

Grandmother makes sure that every six months Bila the painter cleans the gutter poles and paints our fence white. Grandmother grows fiery red roses. Others in Peace Flats grow spinach.

The Tejpars live in a pink four-storey building, they call it Pink Desert. Pink Desert on Royal Ascot. *(Khoti's is a red brick house.)* No one from Peace Flats has ever been to Pink Desert. Kartar Singh lives opposite the Tejpars. A man from France came to build his house. It is white with coloured windows like the windows of European worship houses. Mother Hadhari says that Kartar Singh secretly practices European religion. She says she wouldn't mind if someone died in the Tejpar family. "This way, I can see the Pink Palace. With my right eye, all this talk about the marble floors and turquoise birds from China. Pay my respects to the deceased." She says this to anyone in Peace Flats, even Grandmother.

"The hag's heart grows grimmer with age," Grandmother responds.

In Peace Flats, we call Mrs. Tejpar half-European. Her skin is so pale you can see thin blue veins. She wears hats to match her dresses. And no one laughs at her like you wouldn't laugh at a European wearing a hat.

Once Indu wears a peach-coloured hat with a dotted ribbon around its brim. It's after school and many of us are in the Library garden eating groundnuts. Khoti is sitting on the fence talking with Amin Syed. He has tied his kerchief around his forehead. And his purple socks. Though we are only supposed to wear white socks at School. During inspection time, Miss Chinua just shakes her head and smiles at him. Khoti spells her dictionary words with unsquashy calm.

Indu is on the Library steps. That's when I see her with her hat. We ogle. Then everyone starts laughing. I feel embarrassed for her like you feel when someone forgets their lines in a play. But in five minutes or less, Zul, Mrs. Tejpar's son, brakes in front of the steps, and in full view, Indu climbs into his red jeep.

But Grandmother isn't annoyed at all. She says something strange, "Maybe now we will have a real Heer-Ranjha love story, right here, Peace Flats style. Pity the girl is so vacant." And then Grandmother begins to clean our house. Although it isn't six months since the fence has been painted, she calls Bila. Juma rubs furniture with Mansion Polish. Guest plates are taken out. *(All guests eat out of guest plates at our home.)* They are imported. Grandmother bought them from a British woman returning to London. They have a gold rim. The small centre is white. The rest is a thick border of clustered flowers.

The small nets to cover glasses are re-washed, ready. Normally if someone wants to pluck some roses for the mosque or temple, Grandmother is most willing though she will do the cutting herself. But now she won't allow anyone near her roses.

In a couple of days Mrs. Tejpar's pink car with silver wings stops at our door.

"About time," Grandmother says.

"Mrs. Tejpar at our house?"

"About time."

But as soon as the chauffeur opens his door, Grandmother and I both know that Mrs. Tejpar is not in the car. Even then, before opening the door, Grandmother slips on a fresh apron. Calmly she talks to the chauffeur, accepting a soft linen-like envelope. I can't hear because my ears have gone thick. The chauffeur speaks with hands behind his back and lowers his neck to a bow before departing.

"You mean eat food with her? Why?"

"I'll know on Thursday."

Though I know Mrs. Tejpar has invited Grandmother because of the Zul-Indu *chakker*. She wants Grandmother to bring down their whirling-*chakker* romance. But I daren't ask Grandmother any questions directly.

"Is it because you built the Peace Flats Library?"

"I am one of the founding members of the Library, Child."

"Is it because you are on the Town Council?"

"I am an elected member."

I get bolder, "Did we clean the house because Mrs. Tejpar was going to be here?"

"Nothing is wasted, Child."

On Thursday, Grandmother wears a long cotton dress. Her shawl has butterflies. She waits for the pink car. *(First Khoti's brick house, Pink Desert further up.)*

It is thrilling to know that Zul from the Tejpar family wants to marry Indu of Peace Flats. Zul is "London-Returned." When anyone comes back from London or Germany or Switzerland, always, always, we call them "London-Returned." Their faces aren't tanned any more. Pale and slightly green, even their arms. Their watches are huge and complicated as a diver's. European-style, Zul puts his arm around Mrs. Tejpar's waist when they cross the street. When Indu puts her arm around Mrs. Kassam, Mrs. Kassam snatches her waist away from Indu's grip. And Indu doesn't go to Ramson's anymore. She goes to the Eden where English films are played. A lot of men go to the Eden for the late show when they play: *One Silver Dollar*, *Psycho*, *Frontier Gun*, *Dr. Zhivago*, and *Kentucky Fried Movies*. Indu's flying European walk makes her hair fly back. At the Library she reads *The Wild Cat* and *Sanchez Tradition*, in the open. The *jawans* don't follow her anymore. Only The Poet. The Poet has always been Indu-crazy. His voice slow-deep, tense, and in the Library garden, he recites his favourite verse.

In the desert, Heer searched for her Ranjha
with such a shriek
such a shriek
that God shook, descended instead
Heer said
said Heer to the Creator
"But you are not my Ranjha."

Indu's Poet has no cheeks. Mother Hadhari says, "The poor lad lost his cheeks sucking the juice out of words." His is one house Mother Hadhari never visits. At school bets are made: The Poet will hang himself now. He doesn't. One day, he takes sand from the ground that Indu has just walked on and sprinkles it on his head. Then he does something strange. He goes to live beyond Peace Flats. No one has seen him in town since.

Even though Mrs. Tejpar wants Grandmother to make Indu stop seeing Zul, I bring Zul and Indu together. Then Khoti. . . .

"But you will help Zul and Indu, won't you Grandmother?"

"Child, how dare you squeeze your voice in adult matters?"

Mother Hadhari says to me, "Come Child, come sit beside me."

"Maa Hadhari, Mrs. Tejpar says it's a risk! O Allah bestow more risks so that deserving folk can move up? What's left? Nyerere has taken it all! No, he won't be able to push this Indian around. As if independence swirled only black navels! Bloody independence, Black or nothing! I have slogged too hard to return to farming co-ops. And share profits, *hah*! The Mao bastards. I swear, for Shil, I won't settle for anything less than a gold groom, UK returned. My Shil, so superior to Indu. That silly Kassam girl, mercury quick in disclaiming her tea and spinach heritage, but utterly vacant!"

Grandmother turns her eyes towards me. "Open your ears, Shil, if I catch you doing any mischief, I will cut you limb by precious limb."

Her fury startles me. But I am also flattered. I am put beside Zul and Indu.

Although Indu knows people are talking about her, she is calm. She drinks Coca-Cola in a glass full of cubes with a slice of lemon. The Canteen waiter will do anything for her.

It is Zul "who prances about like a pink monkey in heat," Mother Hadhari says. She is at our doorstep before the eight o'clock school bell, "Grandmother of Shil, come out to the front door, that monkey in heat is at the Kassam's doorstep, suitcase and all!"

The next afternoon, when I come home from school, I see a dusty rose wedding invitation from Pink Desert. Grandmother is cutting roses. She is wearing her five gold bangles. She only wears the bangles on *Idd*.

Khoti is my partner since Meena Pali has malaria. I don't want Khoti to know I like him so I ask Miss Chinua to change my partner.

After Form II, girls and boys sit together. I give her an explanation that is satisfactory. I want to sit with another girl. Miss Chinua tells me just this week, please. I ignore Khoti.

During recess, Amin Syed lays a newspaper in front of me and points to the advertisement.

"What's this?"

"A box of biscuits," although I know very well what the box contains.

Khoti knocks off the newspaper.

"Go ask your sister," he says to Amin Syed.

I stare at Khoti. His skin isn't like Juma's. It's brown like a mango bark with red speckles. Why did Amin Syed have to do this to me in front of Khoti? And I blurt out, my first sentence to Khoti, "You *too* were on this, weren't you?"

Amin Syed balances a bucket of water on the door sill and as soon as Mr. Hali pushes the door, the bucket tilts. Mr. Hali asks us, three times, who the culprit is, and when we do not respond, he asks us to hold out our right palms. Because my palm ducks, Mr. Hali firmly takes my palm and only when the cane is close, he lets it go. Miss Chinua comes in after he finishes. She asks us to read quietly for the remainder of the afternoon.

When no one is looking, Khoti takes out his head-kerchief and dabs some water on it from the bottle he carries (he never drinks tap water). Then on a piece of paper, he writes, "Show me your palm." I do. It has welts on it. Then he cancels out what he has written and writes, "Dab this on," and points to his head-kerchief. The whole afternoon, I keep wetting the kerchief and cover my throbbing palm. And when our knees touch under the desks, we let them be stuck, but on top pretend we don't know.

At home, Grandmother sees my welts.

"How dare the boy not own up? And where was your tongue, Child?"

Grandmother doesn't understand our student pledge to one another. Sort of like the loyalty of the Indian *jawans* to one another. Other classes watch us with admiration. They talk in groups when anyone of us passes. We are the class that wouldn't flitch on our class fellow.

But I tell Grandmother how Khoti helped me keep my palm cool although, "His palm even had a light bubble in the middle."

"I better use the phone at the Library and let Mr. Kamanga know. Just in case the foolish lad takes his class loyalty a bit too far and not let his father know."

The throb in my palm is sweet.

"The School Committee is going to hear on this. That Mr. Hali is welcome to abuse his own kids, but not mine. Shil, you want to invite Khoti for lunch, on Saturday?"

Grandmother makes *khir* with peeled almonds and raisins. And coconut rice with fish. Juma, early in the morning, goes to the market to pick the chicken. Roast chicken marinated in yogurt. But my ears go red when I see the set table. Khoti doesn't know that our real guest plates have not been set. Juma is in the doorway, staring at us. But I don't look at him. The glasses are turned upside down to keep off the flies. But no net coverings.

Grandmother shows Khoti the roses.

Juma still gives me his hard stare. When Khoti asks if he can also thank Juma for the meal, Grandmother doesn't call Juma to the dining room as is proper. We hear whooping laughter and the noise of hand smacking from the kitchen, and Grandmother says, "They are doing their laughter."

I want to get out of the house as soon as possible and ask Grandmother if Khoti and I can ride my bike.

The bike is in the ironing room. Juma and Khoti are in the kitchen. But when I go into the ironing room, Juma is already there. He grabs me and yanks up my skirt.

"You like Black Boys?"

I try to pull down my skirt but he is too strong.

"What's the matter? Indian stick no good?"

"Where is Khoti?"

"In the dining room. You want to find out if his black stick is laden, eh?"

When I yell for Grandmother, Juma covers my mouth and rams me to the wall with his shoulder. Now his face is above mine and I can see the wet lines on his neck.

"Flabby Indian capitalist can't even please his woman now the

Government has taken away his property — *La!* Your Grandmother's cunt would smart if she knows what I know ways-a-way back, eh Shil? Tell her!"

His hand scratches my thighs when I struggle to tear it away and when he reaches the front of my panties, Juma bunches the material and thrusts it inside me. He whispers in my ear. Then he throws me towards the door.

I can't pee because it burns too much. Khoti is unaware happy. He lives on Royal Ascot. I like him this way, black as a nut on the outside but white European inside. Grandmother's selection of groom, only Khoti isn't Indian. But I am not completely like Grandmother. Juma knows all along, what he says in my ear before he throws me out of his ironing room, "Indian-stick not strong for you, eh Shil?"

Queen Bee

They are finally opening the lion-door! It is brick-red and boarded with metal strips. Now for a full seven days and a full seven nights, the door will remain wide open. During the rest of the three hundred and fifty eight days, the ordinary brown door, built within the lion-door is used. We never bother to varnish the ordinary door.

Our house is an enormous U. On the right side of the lion-door is Grandfather's office, where the filing cabinets are pulled out because the cats sleep in them. Grandfather files everything on the three spikes on his tea-stained desk, even carbon paper, which he folds four times then pierces. Any spike will do. Next to the office is the well with its rusty green water, followed by eight bedrooms, and finally, *Maji's* bedroom where she keeps her high steel cupboard.

There is a wide swing in *Maji's* bedroom. Four people can sit on it. *Maji* peels the evening vegetables on the swing and when Munshi Sahib, our goldsmith, comes to show her an intricate pearl necklace, they sit on the swing and view its setting. "*Bibiji*," he tells her, "this piece is the latest design from Begum's Khazaana on Delhi's Khas Chowk. See how these cluster of pearls open like a lotus in sapphire blue water, that's Akbar the Great's design, and *Bibiji*, let me tell you, in jewellery stores in Delhi today, the Moguls have returned."

On the left side of the door is our flour mill. Then an eastern toilet, which I like the best because when I squat, I can feel the churning noise of the mill travelling up my legs. But if I want to read comics, I go next door to the western toilet.

In the curving loop of our U house is the kitchen, storage rooms, Grandfather's rose bins, the outside sitting-room where the sewing machine is, and more storage rooms.

The lion-door joins the two arms of our U house, and to open it fully, half is pushed to the left and half to the right, just like a middle hair parting. Five keys are required to open it. The keys are thick and six inches long, and have patches of rough orange in them. They are kept in *Maji's* steel cupboard with the gold, passports, and currency. *Maji* even has American dollars in her steel cupboard.

The fasting month almost over. Grandfather, *Maji*, and I wait up in the outside sitting room to witness the new moon rise. *Maji* has caked my hands with henna, for the festival. And when we see the moon of *Idd*, Grandfather pulls me into his lap, and recites, "In the name of Allah, the most beneficent, the most merciful." *Maji's* prayer has force: "Allah is one. He is not begot nor begotten, and Muhammad is His prophet."

Maji fasts for the whole month. Grandfather never fasts and every morning, he brings me a toasted *mofa* in bed. I like to wipe my buttery hands on the blanket.

The lion-door remains fully open during *Idd*. Everyone wears new clothes for the whole week, and at least three varieties of rice are cooked each day: sweet orange rice, pilaff with lamb chunks and beady raisins, and white rice. Even past midnight, still new creamy sweets are made and set to cool. The air smells of pounded cloves and nutmeg butter.

On the last day of *Idd*, Shabani, our driver, backs the lorry into the gaping door entrance. Shabani, *Maji*, and Grandfather leave for two weeks with gunny sacks of rice and corn to be distributed to friends and family all over the country.

They are opening it! The door rumbles like a lion rising from thick slumber. I push my palms over my ears and my legs jiggle on their own. Four men, two on each side, push the lion-door toward the side walls. One of the men is new. As he pushes, the muscles in his legs move like teeth grinding food.

"Shil, stay away from the door!" *Maji* shrieks from the sitting-room, where she is having her morning tea.

The sky starts as a fat, upright pole when the lion-door is slowly pushed open, but as it grows wider and wider, the sky begins to run, and such a vast, vast blue falls into the entrance of our house. I can even see dark heads bobbing in the market place.

"Shil, you don't have ears?"

As soon as I hear *Maji's* slapping slippers, I duck but she catches my flying hair.

"*Maji*, let me go!" I yell.

"Never listening, never, never! Didn't I tell you to go and have a bath, and how many times?"

"Don't make me bend, *Maji*, you make my panty show!"

"*Hai* Allah, I'll tell you when you have to worry about pressing your legs!"

A chuckling crowd has gathered outside on the road. How could she do this to me? I go limp in her grasp.

In the bathroom, *Maji* squats and slides the steel bucket under the hot water tank. Then, with one straight movement, she yanks off my petticoat.

"Scrub your armpits well," she says. "And child, bring me scissors when you come out, your nails must be cut."

I don't say yes. I don't say no. When the door shuts, I just slide my foot back and forth on a green, slippery patch. There are several such patches all over the bathroom floor. The best way to get even with *Maji* is by having a cheating bath. I don't touch the soap. Instead, I stick my finger in my ear and go "aah-aah-aah," and then wipe off the brown honey coloured wax on my thigh. I pour water on my stomach and watch it trickle down my legs, until I use up all the hot water.

Now I am in a completely different bathroom. Everything is new, rubbery new. There is a yellow tub with yellow soap and yellow flowers. It makes me queasy, like being in a dipping, rising aeroplane. Back home in Dodoma, next to our muddy bathroom with its slippery mildew cakes, was the place where we killed chickens. When you came out of the bathroom, you saw them sprawled headless, and the brown and rust feathers clung to your wet feet.

This bathroom has an undented innocence; undisturbed. In a way it is like *Maji*, for whom nothing has really changed. From undiscovered linings in that maroon, bread-shaped purse of hers, she can still produce another ruby-studded gold bangle on *Idd*. But here, *Idd* is one grand meal, gorged down with tired energy, after the day is done. On this special day, you still do ordinary things, like drive on John Laurie to go to work, or keep a dentist's appointment. One *Idd*, I rushed off to the Plaza after work and sat through the seven o'clock show and the nine o'clock show. *Idd's* moon doesn't appear in Canada. That white sickle shape in a black-drenched sky. Then she (for me, moon is she) looks like a fragile half-bangle, broken by an amorous kiss. Her slender points, sharp, in the kohl sky set the juice of *Idd* to gyrate.

I am having a cheating bath in this bright bathroom. This time, the water runs in sly rivulets over my stomach before disappearing into the dark down. The bathroom remains oblivious, airy and lemony.

Everyone is still asleep. In the kitchen, I don't bother with opening the curtains. Let it be quiet for a while longer. Mr. Fulford's red lawn mower hasn't begun its snapping. Ant-flocking to Safeway will start in a few short hours. Through the drawn curtains, a muffled sunshine spreads on the counter.

There is a quick patter of feet and Naseema is in the kitchen.

"*Hai* Allah, on a day like this," she says, "you want to sit in the dark?" and opens the curtains fully.

"Naseema, not completely, please! The sun is hitting my eyes!"

"Sorry — this better?" she asks as she pulls the curtains until they nearly meet in the centre.

"Yes, thanks. *Maji* is awake?" I ask.

"Yes. Praying. I'm making her tea, would you like a cup?"

"Ya."

"So, where did you go last night?" Naseema asks.

"Swimming, and then we saw a film at the Plaza."

"What was on?" she asks as she plugs in the kettle. Her short hair has had the regular Friday night oil treatment. It stands about in spikes and tufts.

"A Fassbinder movie," I answer.

"That leather-clad German's film? Man-man sex, woman-woman sex."

"Well, this one didn't have man-man sex in it."

"Oh." But there is a glint in her eye.

"This film is about a railway master's wife having an affair with a man." Why do I feel I *have* to explain?

"Sex?" Naseema asks.

"In the film or out of the film?" I ask. I know where her mind is moving.

Naseema laughs as she arranges *Maji's* tray. Caught her. I am getting fast with Naseema's and *Maji's* cross-examinations.

"Your tea, Shil," she says, ignoring my question.

"Lots of it!" I angrily shout after her.

There is tension when I come home. Naseema goes out too. Her cropped hair shines sharply. The bangles, the walnut eyes, and the soft pink lips barely covering her teeth look dangerous, like a sword. But I have abandoned this artful ritual for a bulky sweater and a thick pair of socks. It does make my family nervous. Naseema performs the rituals of a good woman, tantalizing, yet a swift hedger, who won't give in until the proper time. Until the proper time, when her hands are heavy with bridal henna.

"Shil, *Maji* wants you," Naseema yells from the top of the stairs.

"*Maji*, what do you want?" I yell back.

"Fista-a, yoou comtho!" *Maji* yells back in her English.

Yes, there is a lot of festive yelling when I come home.

Maji's room smells of Vicks. On her dressing table she has so many bottles of pills and in all colours, even dusty rose. There are *halud* fragrance bottles from Saudi (I don't know how she got these), Chanel No. 5, red Cutex bottles, a green bowl filled with brooches and single earrings, safety pins, pennies, and discarded perfume tops.

"*Maji*, what do you want?" I ask and dive in the bed beside her, flinging all the extra pillows on the floor.

"Child, you came home so late and get up so early?"

"But I slept well and I also drank a glass of milk before I went to bed."

"Good, my child. Milk and spinach are very essential for a woman. Coconut oil on elbows and heels. . . ."

I clamp her mouth. "*Maji*, no lecture."

"Now tell me," *Maji* asks, removing my hand from her mouth, "Lots of these yesterdays and todays, you are going with this Keet."

"K-e-i-t-h."

"Yes, yes, but don't fly away my talk. Where is this And-ruun?"

"Oh, he is around. And *Maji*, when he visits, make *chilas* with coriander chutney for him."

"And you?"

"Oh, I am supposed to cook for him too. Like the heroine in Indian films?"

"What nonsense. You cook something for your guest."

"So much food, just for one person?"

"More dishes on the table give it dignity. Shil, you bring this Keet home sometime, I see him with my own two eyes."

"*Maji*, he is only a friend, and a nice person."

"*Hai* Allah, how can I say a person is bad before I meet him?"

Maji is relaxing. I can tell by the way she stretches herself, as if by looking after Andrew or Keith, preparing food for them, no harm will come to me. What if she ever finds out what happened?

"Shil, you know, I took a good look at that And-ruun's right palm when we were in the garden that day. Child, except for a long life line, he has seen nothing, suffered nothing! Allah, the man's so big, and his hand, smooth as a baby's seat!"

"*Maji*, you didn't say nothing to his face, right?"

"Hah, so now I am an empty vessel desperate to make noise?"

"Well, don't worry," I tell her. "Your other granddaughter won't disappoint you. Naseema will bring home a doctor, seasoned in pearls and Islamic History."

"Shil, why must you journey your hand past the back of your skull to touch your ear? You twist everything. Here, rub some Vicks on this cursed ankle of mine."

I sit at the foot of her bed and place her paining foot on my thigh and massage it with gentle pressure. "*Maa*, do you ever think of our old bathroom?"

Maji replies with a stretch, "I remember that tiny hot water tank in the bathroom. First thing when I rose, I put some coal under the tank, while your Grandfather watered his roses."

"You want to know what I remember *Maji?* Those green slippery patches in the bathroom, they were all over the floor."

"Allah, and those bunchy, thread-like creatures sprouting out of them during the rainy seasons. Never, never will I want to have a bath there again." Then in English, "No way!"

Here, if I ever showed the heritage preservers my old bathroom, like *Maji*, they would find it repugnant. Anyway, heritage here is expected to roll into motion after you have arrived. So you must start from a fluffy, yellow bathroom point of view.

Maji has succeeded. Like a queen bee, she maintains her centre, preserving her family and being preserved. She never loses sight of this, not even when Grandfather died. She only said she didn't want the swing in her bedroom anymore. And she didn't break, even when the mill was nationalized and Grandfather's pink roses were blown off by Black Tanzanians, who wanted to show us Indians who was the boss. No one knows how things disappeared from her steel cupboard to reappear in Canada. The maroon purse has taken over where the steel cupboard left. *Maji* is the hub. Everyone works towards her, pleasing her, like Naseema who picks Shiseido lipsticks from Bay sales for *Maji*, the queen bee. Only I have the perfect weapon. My wound would perish her.

I don't do it with Andrew or Keith. It is during my three-month sabbatical as I call it, when I visit India for the first time. When I swoosh Ganges in my mouth, I secretly wait for Small *Maji*, my rusty, African water. Waiting in ochre India, place of meetings, for my legacy to sediment. Ganga-Ganges is generous. There is a story of a sage who prayed to Ganga to flow down to earth because the parched earth was cracking. Kind Ganga agreed but her powerful rush would sweep away the earth. God Shiv in the Himalayan mountains interceded, and she flowed to earth from Shiv's hair knot, unrushed, cool and kind. In Ganga-Ganges' course, place of meetings, my lineage will swell for I come from a lineage of *Majis*: Ancient Ganges *Maji*, Middle *Maji* married to Grandfather, and Small African *Maji* who gives me birth. But I am husk dry. Only space whistles about my bones, so I must be a ghost. In this land of my ancestors, I recite all names of Ganges the benevolent, "Doe/*mai*/sorrow/salt/wise/clement/*Ganga jal*/holy/udder/lap, gush forth with such moisture that I reek of henna and wet rust." Ganges *Maji* leaves perfunctory marigolds in my mouth.

At various Indian universities, I carefully read the works of Atwood, Birney, Nowlan, Laurence, and Munro, and Webb, working up a heritage. I coax and ply for a feeling to roar inside me. Nothing comes. I commit my suicide then. I do it in Delhi, an old part of Delhi. The freshly eaten food rises in my throat when his weight topples on me. As soon as he has finished, I sit up and duck my head to see. I have not leaked a single drop of blood.

"giving up the company of women"

"(cham cham vaghar)
(rai methi lasann gheema ladhey . . .)
Mustard seeds popping in hot butter
crushed garlic whispering urgent, pungent messages
while fenugreek seeds help amber the butter.
Today I use a wooden spoon
tumeric stained,
we let the garlic take over the house before
opening the windows. Let the mustard seeds fly
as far as they dare"

And this for Ondaatje *Babu* of *Running in the Family*

A cupped *salaam* is for God and guests but I swear on Allah
in your eyes Ondaatje *Babu*, slippered elephants sway.

When Rushdie *Saab* comes home,
I will knead flour with flying fingers
but you *Babuji*
I will feed anciently, trembling food on my long fingernail

Among crazed eyebrows furring thick to ward off the Tundra
Babuji, there crept your Sri Lankan eyebrows, silk mild
then two eyes cinnamon smudged. I died.

Readerji, my *Readerji*, I have selected these quotes, writers and compositions to draw you to my craft as a story-maker and a language-maker. I create from she-space, food, and romance: "romancing man," "romancing Allah," and "romancing baby." *Readerji*, if you are aghast about my romance with a baby, then substitute "romancing baby" with "nurturing baby." Romance is my tongue *politique*. Also, I am known as an "Other-writer," an "Outside writer." I am not of mainstream caste but my Overseer-Husband belongs to this high caste.

Enough of this meandering or as my *Guruji* van Herk would say, "If you bring a gun into your story, it must go off by the end of the story, what's your point?" Nothing really. I'll goof off because she isn't here. Seriously *Readerji*, I am tired of approaching "Other literature" from the viewpoint of the colonizer. To explain, to translate, to ask my Overseer-Husband, "*Husbandji*, am I explaining within the confinement magistrated by Vous?" *Readerji*, what to do? He has paid my bride price; now I have been granted a dark blue passport. Now I travel visa-free to most countries because of *Husbandji's* book/seal/clout. Airport officials greet me, "From Canada, eh? No problem." Stamp stamp. "Have an enjoyable stay." In the same airports, the line marked "Third World" is full of shuffling.

But my blood is hibiscus red and I crave romance. So I romance with cunning. I swear *Readerji*, that there is enough friction-fiction between *Husbandji* and I for a torrid romance. It begins with *Husbandji* calling me, Other.

In mainstream literature, the celebration of Other has been encouraged in recent years: Other-texts, *gurujis*, writing workshops, funding agencies, global awakening, conferences. It is the season of the Other, "Please, after you, after you," I am ushered on mainstream's promenade deck. And especially these *maha* hyphenated-magicians, writing back from the Raj-*wallah*-Empire. These magicians parted the East West sea. To call these magicians prophets would blunt their glory. Now, the immigrant can go back and forth, shamelessly collecting along the way. The parting, call it sea parting or hair parting or margin is packed too close. These *maha* hyphenated-magicians' *istyle*, superbly western but their content ground for an *asli*-authentic burp/pleasure: spicy-yellow-sour-loud, no apology. I speak of Salman Rushdie and Hanif Kureshi, the clan-*wallahs* of Other writing. But there are others and I get impatient when texts by lesser known pen-*wallahs* are not incorporated into the school syllabi, more speedo, *fatafat, chapa chapa*. I welcome established *pen-wallahs* like R.K. Narayan and Anita Desai, but I have had enough. I want Sujata Bhatt, Sara

Suleri, Gita Mehta, Debjani Chatterji, and Sky Lee. By the way, *Readerji*, this talk-talk with you is not a manifesto of any kind. It is my desire/romance with mainstream/*Husbandji*, not sinister hand salute/ declaration. Red book and sickle. Lenin died last year. I saw a photograph of fallen Vladimir in a magazine. It's okay to use his first name. He has an oval profile (not a massive lion head jutting out of truncated neck). A young man in a bisque coloured walking shoe (not a fur-hatted Russian shoe) crushes Vladimir's insuperable oval chin. Why are you getting impatient, *Readerji?* What do you mean, "so?" It means freedom; it means going crazy for imported yuppie shoes and getting them in KGB Russia! Yes, yes, *Readerji*, I know the massive country has broken up.

I know a manifesto means freedom, only now. And still, I finger its texture distrustfully. It is smooth but means a machine gun, many machine guns. It means the colour red and dehydrated milk and shortage of bread and I wave a flag (red again) when Tito visits Tanzania in 1974. I run around the school compound, singing slogans out of a chaffed voice-box, taught by President Nyerere. He licks freedom promised by communist *muftis*, Mao and Tito.

butcher the enemy
kill America capitalist
join *ujamaa* village
brother to brother sharing
individual property
who says is yours, you Indian mooch?
your knicker is not your knicker
Indian lice-parasite
give me five
this is communism!

I remember the thin, tall Canadian who interviews us. So many times, mother repeats the story of the tall officer who places immigration papers in her lap. Many are rejected and many receive their forms across the table. Mother repeats how his tall body bends to place freedom in her lap. Over the years, she traces him a gray suit, sometimes charcoal, even green. She does not give him European eyes. They are almond shaped like an Indian beauty's. Her tall sun (he surpasses son) is a lifter and feeder. It is balmy in the north for mother. Nowadays she blushes when she thinks of her sun-son. Tender memories fattened with age, and

At the airport in Dar es Salaam
our hems ripped
East Indians, like dogs
tail between legs
suitcases tied with silly ropes
our entry to the West

Is this word "manifesto" a trend, lately? My friend, the word is terribly male. Male history (Lenin just died but I can't get over Mao, Tito, and Nyerere) and catchy tunes for the proletariat. Don't rough it about manifestos over cafe au lait. I have lived it, under Brother Nyerere, gun, and sexual harassment.

In 1974
an African touched my breast
On the street
I walk with
hunched shoulders

My female rejects the word. "Manifesto" is a *mard*/male/*mwanamume*/*poto* command when I like the breath of a male behind my ear, on my navel, and on my breast when I empower/pull his hand. But I write my own language, my own declarations, full of chatter of wine fingers, of perfume gone sour after exhilaration.

The erection of "males write about the real thing" is bunk, bunk, first-class bunk. I, a woman story-maker, want to disturb such an erection, just like, how can gun and central control become trendy? And one more thing, I want to bring the word "*mufti*" into circulation, so that each time the word pops up on TV (albeit delivered with flare) you do not dive into your burrow, screaming, "Terrorism, terrorism!" Of course, words like *mufti* or *umma* occupy almost all space in Islam and gender is specific: male. But by plaiting such prerogative words into my stories, I begin to disturb their weight. As you see, dear *Readerji*, I, woman story-maker, waffle with cunning.

Give credit where credit is due. Isn't it a hoot when a Muslim heroine's clothing burns, leaving her first-class naked, except for her chiffon *duppata*/scarf, which remains unsinged, floating and shy-eyed, protecting our virgin (of course!) heroine's modesty? Pity this *pen-wallah*, Rushdie *Babu*, is male!

Now I am ready for my cafe au lait.

Personally, my relationship with mainstream has been fresh. Oh no, *Readerji*, don't take "fresh" literally! Not in the sense of fresh cut flowers, fresh lettuce, fresh cream. Don't go to the green grocer. Waffle with me, *Readerji*. Fresh in the sense of new and exciting, out of our friction, *Readerji*. *Husbandji* is a *baanka chora*. City boy. He wears silk trousers and goes about slotting things according to his pocket watch. And I, *Readerji*, waffle with cunning. This is our love chapter.

I am not naive to *Husbandji's* dominant power to anthropologize "what is ethnic?" and what type of text-product he expects. In a comic strip, Mr. Colonizer (khaki shorts, helmet, camera, and pipe) is spotted in a boat by "natives." Next thing, the "natives" are frantically rowing homeward, warning each other, "Hide the videos! Hide the videos!"

Then there is the "ethnic story" demanded by a local newspaper in a story competition. Well, I don't want to be this type of Other writer. The poor-Other, clad in a widow's white sari who can only have one scrawny meal a day without garlic (without garlic!) until first-class, *baanka chora*, Canada dry *Husbandji* rescues her. How *Husbandji* shivers and his veins swim in red ecstasy when the widow sings weird blood-praises of her husband country. *Yaar-Readerji*, you are shocked! Foreplay is the hush-hush secret to pleasure a lover and the widow is a professional *Husbandji's* way — a song in which *Husbandji* comes out a hero-saviour and the widow's *jati*/caste/country is nothing but dung and bunk until the rational, strong hero *Husbandji* takes over. If the widow sings blood-praises of her husband-country she left because her breast wants no other touch and in her womb, never a foreigner's seed, that's her freedom/choice. Fine, and I don't call her a widow, but a woman with two husbands, and in my religion as woman, I allow it, for my woman-person thrives on many romances: baby romance,

Allah romance, man romance, woman romance. In the moist garden, I stretch slow-slowly. My warm bangles slide back and nudge a cool patch of skin.

But when I am forced to breed in a language, gem/gene selected by mainstream *Husbandji*, fostering, glorifying, encircling and churning out a pressed vision, than I the Other, dry/die. Then the widow/ story-maker is compelled to burn on her husband's funeral pyre, forced to leap into the fire by mainstream caste. Then her suicide and his murder are perfectly mated. *Readerji*, witness the horror of such perfection: this time, the pyre the icy Bow, the husband, a Punjabi, dominant in his family. He wants sons, she (so insignificant, she does not deserve a name nor introduction) produces a son but the child dies of cancer. The husband demands sons/circumscription, so

woman after three girls
this fourth, another wretched girl
threw one by one
into icy Bow
wife-woman, girl-women
and baby-woman
dead one spring
Calgary, 1 May, 1979

My groom-*Husbandji*, let me write freely without ethnic expectations, your powerful caste demands. Don't file me under a category which has dusty arms in anthropology and the flat factuality of sociology. I am a story-maker and I will tell you of a husband I dreamed of on an Indian rooftop. *Readerji*, do you know the story of the bamboo flute? She is blue Krishna's mistress.

She
bamboo flute
held between lover's lips
(lover's grasp
tough as mother's womb)
the lover has forgotten
other shapes. All.

"That kept one"
Radha sniffs.
Everyone on rooftop knows
that without Radha
there is no Krishna.
so what if he is a god?
(*Radha bina Kanu nahi*)
but even Radha
says to her Kanu
"tear that wretched bamboo
from your mouth
place *her* at your foot."
Bamboo flute/other/eternally
torn from siblings
holed in peak flesh
for one beloved's breath.
When blue Krishna
billows inside her
her breast holes sting
she reels
higher than bells.
Such romance
out of rooftop
full of tears succulent.
It is on rooftop
a lover is made
most perfect
then pressed behind eye
and the wind on rooftop
sweeter than Chinook.

I have a rooftop here, I swear, bracketed, dreamy: Trudeau or Pierre? Shy choice. But I fetch you, green coat (collars dashed up), colour of powdered henna, in the pink city of Jaipur. Red rose.

Readerji, see, I am footloose, out of reach of *Husbandji* and his octopus grabber caste, but there are other realities I have to contend with. Now, I feel like Buddha contemplating under the Bodhi tree. But then, there is nothing lofty about journeys being a modern immigrant's religion. In fact, an immigrant's other name is Nomad, grasping settlement in terms of movement only. Then I/Other/nomad/immigrant am in celebration — of course, a lonely celebration. It is the time when my senses pick up the peculiar/eerie. These vibrations/seismographs show up on my nomad's graph. They are blue as a bruise — how nomads are kissed. Once, I am pelted with blue kisses.

"Out, out of here, *tout suite*, *pronto*, *fatafat*, *chapa chapa*," a washerwoman shouts at me. To her, I am the pariah/*firangi*/foreigner/out/oust caste, mixed and polluted everywhere: no heritage, no history. Even the Ganga couldn't cleanse me. But the blue kiss creates my fiction. Location: Delhi.

Away from the wash cycle, I sleek my body (special effect) to a sleeker Italian capsule (red). Glide engineless through John Laurie: bank, cheese, phone bill (a forty-five minute press). But now, out of industrial design, out of circumscription/orbit, I am on visa, in Delhi, where I make love poems.

There is a gully-womanizer who walks up and down the winding gully, which is full of *hakims*, dyers, tea stalls, urine salt on walls, book marts, kosher stalls, Asha Bhosle's guttural couplets from *Umrao Jan*. Yes, there is a cinema packed in a gully, marigold baskets, mullah's *azan*, Shiv dancing on white tiles, banyan tree. I can't find room for cows and auto-rickshaws in my list, but one thing in a gully, women tamper on the way to the temple. The most beautiful look down, part of poetics. Back to gully-womanizer who has a brisk head-shape. His curls, dark and full mouthed. His *yaar*-friends call him Guru for his Ghalib gestures. (Phyllis *Bibi*, our Canadian *pen-bibiji*, got tired of Ghalib's soggy wine and women. She yanked him off her typewriter with something like, "Oh, quit whining on women and wine. Go drink tea! Sober up!") *Hai* Allah, *Readerji*, that day there so much talk-talk on rooftop! Of course, I on the rooftop with my *sakhi*-friends, send her a few couplets, right back:

Bibiji, you finished Ghalib so fast: wine, women, politics
Didn't you hear a bamboo tear? A ghost flute mistress

Your pen, as yet milk teeth
amoured by Urdu contours, seductive rollings left to right

Didn't you hear *Mian* Ghalib's calligraphy Otherly hungry?
Shudder/murder?

Milk teeth *Bibiji*, your couplet is done,
go play outside.

Readerji, our gully-womanizer is of Ghalib-caste. This is the ripe truth. See how he bends (left hand to chest) and spreads sand on his hair. Awesome compliment to the woman he bends for. But of course, she won't look up. (That's Madame Umrao Jan's profession, to raise her right hand to the middle of her forehead, bend her beauty head, and recite a throaty "thankyou*janaab*-admirer.") Such is the way of Delhi. *Readerji*, don't say Delhi, say "Dilhi," all in the mouth, tip of tongue to roof. "Dilhi," it is a French kiss.

At the Hotel Imperial, I take my feet to the hairdresser. Under the Babul tree, I read, true almond is a member of the rose tree. Almonds and roses—*Readerji*, these are very familiar to an East Indian woman. Stand in the doorway with almonds and roses. This is the way to bid a guest welcome. And after meal of *nan*, pilaff, mutton, chicken, and vegetables in thick sauce, place mangoes beside a guest. Since it is impossible to place nearly all of the three thousand varieties of mangoes, don't forget to place the most expensive Alfonsos from Maharashtra. Langdas from Uttar Pradesh are another lush offering. And finally, upon an unhasty completion of the mangoes, set a finger bowl decked with a string of jasmines in front of a guest. Pile Baroque thickness, such is the way to treat a guest. To treat a man. *Readerji*, the guest/man ties the string of jasmines to his wrist. His immense face (it appears immense to me) softens as it turns toward my *zenana* quarters. Yes, flowers are strung in the *zenana* and sent over to the guest/man's abode. Such formality between a woman and a man/guest and the business of sweet stringing. For this way, a man curbs a woman, by making her speech (she never speaks) and space exotic.

But a female is never a guest. She sits with me on the rooftop where I dye veils, green as bangles, sometimes mustard, and of course pink, full of Saturday night dreams. With a man, a woman speaks his language of flowers. Woman wallows in self-indulgence, a wonderful mud only in the company of women.

In an Indian film, the heroine quivers like a turquoise kingfisher, but deft in diving out of the hero/guest's eye, *tout-suite, fatafat, pronto.* Such is a good woman in a sage's story or a mother-in-law's manifesto. One of the bride's sixteen bridal pieces is the art of how to vanish. *Readerji*, you are familiar with another of her bridal pieces, that a beauty does not talk. And she never calls the hero by his name. She calls the hero, *Him*, third person. Such formality and simultaneous intimacy. A rushed name in the beloved's ear, only in their balmy chamber.

Child-woman colours her secret picture book of her groom-prince. Seasoned Hero (Marlboro Man) smiles. He knows it is he who will flood her red. He will flood her red when she brings him a glass of milk. The heroine sings that in waiting for *Him*, she has become senseless like Krishna's Radha. Marlboro Man smiles. (Didn't Radha curse Krishna that in her next birth, the Blue God be Radha and suffer her plight? And she, Krishna.) Violence, passion, bowing at a man's lotus feet. These are a woman's jewels, crafted on her, since birth. You have only to know how to read the bridal pieces, *Readerji*. But the heroine has seen the hero! Whoosh! Disappears! Like a good woman. Now it is the man-groom-prince's duty to hunt her down. In fairy tales, this is saving the princess.

Maybe I have had too much Kingfisher. (*Readerji*, there are other beers beside Molson Canadian.) My eyelids are heavy as thighs. Do you know, that in thighs there is saffron, breasts, and milk? A wife's bangles shimmer as she packs blanched almonds in the nightly milk for her husband. Only then to enter their balmy bed chamber.

There is a cat under my lawn chair. Even then the crow swoops low and takes a bow. Crow, take a message as you do in daughter stories. Tell my mother I am happy under the Babul tree. Babul home is a girl's home before marriage.

There is a washerwoman who banishes me from Delhi. I can still hear her clamour. "Quick, out of here, *fatafat* (clap, clap), *tout suite!*"

Your foreign woman blood, a bleat of blood, husk-dry in three days." (Who told you so?)

"Ours bleed lustily, so dark, it gives off purple. Purple as a Java Plum." (I forget whether the mango or plum is sacred.)

Frizzy hair (left open) and airy breasts are worse. Worse still is an unfastened Indian woman. Not fastened to my woman neck two gold nuggets (heavy droops of ruby nipples). An Indian-Kamla-comely has breasts full of a tigress' milk.

Outside the Earth Sciences Building, I ask Nicole, "Can so many risks fit inside my woman?" From Kensington on bike, she flexes her shins and does her Winnipeg riddle speech, "If I say yes, then where are the risks? Yet, I cannot say no, for they are not invisible. Between this yes and no, your risks course your woman map." Her eyes without almond spoof. But wacky green. I fall in love with Nicole then and on lilac hedges that day, it is a summer of mangoes. Washer-woman, you will never know of Nicole who washed my blue nails. What do you know of familiar secrets that crush the heart (again) like a whistling stone from a catapult? No, I will never reveal to you Nicole's prairie long hair — that flick of her palm, now a mango knot. Mango, a goddess' favoured fruit.

Readerji, once I am circumcised. I have innocence and blaze implanted in my eye. (It is an ancient operation.) I receive early credentials in eye-lock practice. But I leave my sakhi-eyes inside the circle. All good women reside inside the circle, learning devotion and heady eyes. And in marriage, good women receive two gold nuggets (heavy droops of ruby nipples). But I leave the circle for *Ji*. That day, there is bitter weeping in the *zenana*. I have brought shame. In a parking lot in London, another woman is hacked to pieces by her father because she brings shame to her tribe. She brings shame/ *sharum/besharum*, unfastening herself for an English boy. Out of her looms Rushdie's Sufiya Zinobia in *Shame*. Such stories of woman shape/shame.

I want to tell *Ji*, "You and I should have stopped at the heart." In my dream, I sit mother on the toilet. She has no arms or legs. Her shriek so bitter, that in the dream, I leave *Ji*, forever.

A heroine has almond eyes. Dove-tender. In the *zenana*, she is taught to speak with flowers. She is taught to wine her eyes. How to tease and hedge, blameless as milk. Ancestral practice carried on in a daughter's quarter, until the time, when folded in sixteen pieces of jewellery, she moves toward prince-groom.

I leave my sakhi-eyes inside a circle. Husband-Yes-A-God, *Devi* Sita practices. (That's how she become a *Devi.*) In the forest where Lord Rama and *Devi* Sita exiled for fourteen years, Lakshman follows. Lakshman is Rama's half-brother but a true brother, another moral in the story. When the brothers go on a hunt, Rama leaves Lakshman with the secretarial duty of drawing a protective line around Sita. (A woman inside a circle is cherished.)

Man and wife apart in public. Third person formality. In old fashioned stories, the mother-in-law instructs her daughter-in-law, "take him milk." (In private Ram calls Sita, Situ. In private I call him *Ji.*)

I am a Sita-woman once, and a circle drawn around me with the good stuff: henna, cinnamon bark, even strawberries, from the Okanagan Valley. When my nipples are wormy protrusions, I learn to pour milk on the phallus-*lingam* and the housewife economy of killing a snake without breaking the stick. When I step out of the circle not guileless like Sita who is abducted by Ravan-monster, mother calls me a whore.

With a Swiss Army knife, *Ji* cuts tender lamb pieces for me. The smell of newspapers curls out of the food. His stomach still red from the meat ovened under his *kurta* as he hurries to my door step. And when he leaves, he draws a circle around me, in a scanty Delhi room, where I make love poems.

There is this exile/blue kiss (one end of the sea) and exile and romance (other end of the sea).

Coyote, Atwood, maple red on white
prairies on and on
(haven't ever had saskatoon berries).
Bears out there
wear bells,
rocks run blue
after their blueberry feast in fall.
At the Conference in Delhi
how I filch
credit for the Rockies
strut them personally as breasts

my padshah host beams
"from Canada, how you say,
eh, no?"
c'est moi
international poster. Seducer.

Readerji, then there is Canada-*dulhan*, northern bride. I am not talking about Canada-dry Husband*ji*, the colonizer. There is also a vast bride. She is selected by the (dominant) immigrant for her sturdy haunches, rich dowry. Canada-woman-north-bride asks her immigrant husband:

Never to ask me, ME
an arranged wife
your hostile giving
to my blue passport band.
Egg shell virginity
between you and I
mosaic hymen.

Readerji, is this binary inevitable? One is the colonizer, the other, the colonized. Then whoa, whoa *Readerji*. Now, please pick up speed and move! *Chapa chapa, tout-suite* (clap clap), *fatafat*, out of my text because I shy/sly from any confinement/circle/missionary position. Friction/fiction between mates facilitates ousting of hierarchical positions. I don't want to be the sturdy alphabet to set a novice at ease in Other literature — a vaccination prior to his/her flight into the Third World. But sometimes this has to be done, then I can't help it, especially, when *Husbandji* is so naive, full of milk teeth, as in the case of a "*20/20*" reporter. Benezir Bhutto does a Raj number on him!

With Eastern princess softness
Benezir Bhutto of Oxford and Radcliffe
seduces the reporter —
She must move a tortoise stretch
she explains his smitten teeth,
while forgotten women in Karachi prison
lick after freedom
she promised them.

Such work is simple, one dimensional but I am compelled (I am a singer and protector) to write lowly — show *Husbandji*, baby step by baby step. But I really want to tango with my mate (want to dance?) I want to push friction in fiction, both in the other, other realm (where the washer-woman kicks me out), and here, to push language crazy, in footloose English. Let me roam-romance. Free! My speech sings *(gayati)*. My speech protects *(trayate)*. I am Gayati, singer/shielder/ romancer.

Readerji, weddings are auspicious, where a bit of you and a bit of me. Come, attend my *sakhi*-friend's wedding on the rooftop. My *sakhi* has gone to the tailor's for wedding measurements. The limbs are differently thick now, that's why we call them wedding measurements.

Don't know why
I turn shy
when my *sakhi*
shows me his photograph.
He wears an earring
and collects Sher-Gill
(Now on *Sakhi* and I call him Sher-Gill *wallah*.)

Readerji, and that is Sher-Gill *wallah's* mum, carrying my *sakhi's* bridal veil, henna, and soil.

I laav you
moi: full of french shoulders
but English "my" lukewarm at the same time possessive
moi: a burst
heart/soil/Saturday night dream
ooi moi changi-kuri girl, *ooi moi* pretty-*soni* girl
all jaunty praise in Punjabi
mustard flowers/couplets/*giddha* dance . . .
but I laav you
Sher-Gill *wallah's* mum says in English

Readerji, dance to my havoc/rock/pitch English. There is Sujata Bhatt frying garlic and mustard seeds, "crushed garlic whispering urgent, pungent messages," that's a bit of me. Now I will follow you into the prairie ice-cream sky, *Readerji*, I crave a bit of you. Garlic and ice-cream. I swear there is enough friction-(sweet) fiction between us. Yes *Readerji*, you and I could certainly be called a love story.

Acknowledgements

Acknowledgement is made to the editors of the following publications in which some of the stories and poems have appeared: *Alberta ReBound, SansCrit, Kasmir, Dandelion, Vox, Secrets from the Orange Couch, The Toronto South Asian Review*, and *The Road Home*. "giving up the company of women," was read at a conference on writing and ethnicity. Almost all pieces in this collection have been revised since their initial publications.

These stories, or earlier versions of them, previously appeared in the following publications:

"Aisha" in *Alberta ReBound*, NeWest Press, 1990
"The Play Begins" in *Vox*. December 1990
"Queen Bee" in *Kasmir*. Volume 2 Number 4, 1990
"Paris in Bombay" in *Secrets from the Orange Couch*.
Volume 2 Number 1, 1990
"Be a Doctor" in *SansCrit*. Volume 2 Number 1, 1990
The poem "Bamboo Mistress" from "giving up the company of women" will be published in *The Road Home* by Reidmore Books Inc. in 1992.
The title "giving up the company of women" is taken from *Meatless Days* by Sara Saleri. Published by the University of Chicago Press in 1989.

The publisher and author gratefully acknowledge the following for permissions to reprint quoted material:

Bhatt, Sujata; "The Garlic of Truth". Copyright © 1988 by Carcanet Press Limited. Reprinted by permission of Carcanet Press Limited.

Gunnars, Kristjana; *The Prowler*. Copyright © 1988 by Red Deer College Press. Reprinted by permission of Red Deer College Press.

Suleri, Sara; *Meatless Days*. Copyright © 1989 by the University of Chicago press. Reprinted by permission of the University of Chicago Press.

Every effort has been made to obtain permission for quoted materials. If there is an omission or error the author and publisher would be grateful to be so informed.

Yasmin Ladha

Yasmin Ladha was born in Mwanza, Tanzania. She immigrated to Canada in 1978 at the age of twenty. Numerous journeys to India, the rich talk-stories of her youth, and the influence of female role models like her mother and grandmother provide a constant energy to her work. Yasmin is currently completing her master's degree in English at The University of Calgary. She has one previously published book, *Bridal Hands on the Maple* (DisOrientation Chapbook, 1992) and has been featured in numerous periodicals and anthologies, including *Alberta ReBound* (NeWest Press, 1990).